The Boy in Makeup

The Boy In Makeup

A NOVELLA BY

ANTHONY CONNORS-ROBERTS

Story by Anthony Connors-Roberts
Illustration: Luna Beasley
Main Editor: Misha Kydd
Other editors: Camila Cardoso
Special thanks to all BETA readers.

DEDICATION BY AUTHOR

*I'd like to dedicate this all the boys in makeup -
Never let anyone dull your sparkle!
And to my husband and son - I love you both.*

Chapters

The Boy In Makeup

Anthony Connors-Roberts was born, brought up and educated in South Wales. He wrote plays and short stories as a teenager and more recently wrote an online blog.

While adopting his son, he worked as a business manager for a makeup brand but was made redundant during covid, so he took time off to be a full-time dad. Many projects followed until he decided to start writing *The Boy In Makeup*. He first uploaded a series of chapters on Tapas, a platform for budding writers. Then Anthony released *The Boy In Makeup* as an Ebook, which to his surprise, reached top of the chart for LGBTQ+ short stories.

Today, Anthony lives with his husband, son and two chihuahua's in Barry, South Wales.

Download the "The Boy In Makeup" Spotify music playlist.

Use your phone camera to scan the link above, or search "The Boy In Makeup" on Spotify.

Cory

I tapped Go LIVE.

I don't know about you, but the thought always makes me anxious.

Before I applied my makeup, I waited around thirty seconds for enough followers to join the live feed. If anyone else were in my room right now, they'd think a little gremlin was lurking around as my stomach was making some odd noises. It's nerves or hunger, or maybe both.

School starts in under an hour, and I should be downstairs having breakfast, but that can wait today because who needs Coco Pops when you can look fabulous instead?

I enjoy being on social media because accessing the world outside Oldport has allowed me to connect to more diverse people, and some enjoy my makeup content. It's a massive confidence boost that four thousand people have subscribed to my TikTok makeup page, but doing a live feed makes me feel slightly sick. I think it's the unpredictability of anyone being able to watch and comment.

'Hi, everyone. I'm doing a quick makeup look,' I said into the phone's front-facing camera lens. 'I thought you could ask me questions so I don't feel daft doing my makeup on camera.'

How old are you? a new follower asked.

'I'm fifteen! Sixteen this August,' I said as I scooped a handful of No7 moisturiser and smothered it on. The cream glistened on my skin as the phone screen illuminated my face.

A pupil from my school asked, Are you staying at Cartridge High or doing college next term?

I sighed. 'I'm definitely not going to stay at Cartridge.'

I'm not too fond of school; I'd much rather apply for a job at a makeup counter, or I might go on and do beauty Level 2 at college. But it would be my idea of hell to stay on at school for another two years.

Cory, are you gay? You're beautiful, OMG LOL! asked an excited, cringe-worthy follower.

'Thanks! Yes, I'm gay. I came out last year but still don't have a boyfriend. I don't think many gay boys will ever fancy me as I like to wear makeup, which many view as being too feminine,' I said as I tapped in some Kiehl's eye cream with my pinky.

A commenter asked, Are you going to this year's Pride?

'Yes!'

Another asked, Fave singer/band?

'Ariana!' I pointed to a poster across the room. My walls were plastered with posters of Ariana Grande and drag queens from RuPaul's Drag Race.

Who's your favourite best friend ever? asked Lizzie.

I chuckled. 'Lizzie, you're my best friend.'

Someone else asked, When did you start wearing makeup?

'Around two years ago.' I started wearing makeup after finding a foundation sample in a magazine. At first, a few of the boys at school teased me, and the head of year asked me not to wear makeup at school ever again, but I still did. Even if it's against the school's "No makeup on boys" policy, I would feel naked without it.

At this point, over two hundred and fifty people had joined the live video chat. I glanced at the growing numbers and my stomach rumbled; thankfully, no one heard.

Do your parents know U R gay? asked a viewer.

'Yeh. I have Mum, but she's fine; she has always known deep down.' I was now applying a light coverage Nars foundation I got for Christmas.

The comments were coming in so fast it was hard for me to catch up with reading the questions before they disappeared. And not all the messages were positive, either – some fake profiles wrote Gay boy! What a bender. This attention made me a little more nervous, but I did my best to ignore it – after all, I was used to being called derogatory names.

But one negative message did get my back up: You tried it on with Lewis Jackson at the house party. You deserve a slap! someone commented.

'Actually,' I quickly responded, 'I'd rather not talk about this. I never tried to kiss anyone; I'm not like that.' I tried to act like the negative comments weren't bothering me, but my hands started to tremble as I applied my Hoola bronzer from Benefit.

Last year I came out as gay to the school. Hardly anyone was surprised, mainly because I had been wearing full-on makeup for a while, and I had never been one of the lads – I'd always hung out with my only friend, Lizzie. Everyone seemed fine regarding me being gay until I went to a house party one weekend. Quite a few people in my year were also there, and once almost everyone had fallen asleep, a popular straight boy, Lewis Jackson, kissed me. I was taken aback by the kiss, and because I pushed him away, Lewis became angry and woke people up to say I was the one who tried it on with him!

That's the thing about when you're gay: some straight boys with toxic masculinity think any gay male will fancy them – and this helped Lewis's false narrative about me at the house party. After this, people teased me in school, making my life much more difficult. I proceeded to do my eye makeup with my Huda Beauty eyeshadow palette.

Messages flooded the comment section:

Who is Lewis Jackson?

Why did you try to kiss a straight boy?

Freak!

The viewer count was now over five hundred people. With the negative messages and viewer numbers growing, I ended the live feed prematurely.

'Guys, I need to go. I have school soon, sorry!' I closed
the live feed and unattached my phone from the tripod.
But it wasn't the Lewis Jackson comments that made me
end the live feed early. The last negative comment was a
trigger; freak is not the worst thing people could call
me, but for some reason, that word hurts deeply.

I looked at myself in the mirror hung above the desk.

'You're not a freak,' I whispered to myself.

Please don't replay that comment on your mind today, I
thought, trying to be kind to myself.

I sat back on my desk chair and took a moment to think
about what had been said. I took a deep breath as I
tried to calm myself down. In front of me, numerous
cosmetics were scattered all over my not-so-white Ikea
desk. Inside my mind, it didn't look much different.

I was no longer starving when I left the house, because I managed to grab a piece of toast on my way out. Still, my washing machine stomach was on a spin cycle as I walked inside the school gates. The gates of hell, I thought to myself.

'Lizzie,' I shouted as my best friend waved in the distance. The first school bell rang, and we both had maths together.

Cartridge High was built in the seventies and hadn't had a refurb since. The place could have done with having a glow-up or being rebuilt again.

'Those idiots on TikTok live… Are you all right?' Lizzie said, concerned.

I explained I was used to the Lewis Jackson backlash and name-calling, and I sounded convincing, but I knew

Lizzie would know the truth even if she didn't say anything.

'Also, there is a boy out there who will love you whether you wear makeup or not, Cory.'

I begged to differ, but I didn't have the energy to debate whether I could get a boyfriend. 'Anyway, I'm dreading the maths test results today,' I said as I tried to avoid the never-going-to-get-a-boyfriend topic.

Lizzie squealed, 'I'm excited about maths.'

'Sure you are.' I chuckled, knowing that Lizzie had probably scored the highest in class because she was one of the top-performing students in our year.

Standing in the hallway, chatting to art teacher, Miss Bush, was head of year Mr Harris, whom Lizzie and I had nicknamed Sergeant Major. I instantly started to panic, like a zebra spotting a hungry lion coming towards them.

'Cory James, what muck is on your face?' Mr Harris shouted in his stern voice. He was built like a rugby player and was a lot taller than Lizzie and me.

'I'm—' I said before being rudely cut off.

'You will wash it off immediately; you are a boy, not a clown!'

Sheepishly, I replied, 'Yes, sir.'

My chest pounded fast, and I was embarrassed about the other pupils overhearing.

Lizzie couldn't believe the way Mr Harris had spoken to me. Although she wished she could stick up for her best friend, she wouldn't ever want to be in the firing line of Sergeant Major.

We walked off. 'Why doesn't Miss Bush ever intervene? Mr Harris can't talk to a student like this; it's so bad,' Lizzie complained.

'I don't know, but I know I need to wash all this off now.' I wished I hadn't applied my makeup so generously that Mr Harris could notice, but I got slightly carried away on the live feed.

'And waste the expensive makeup you've applied? What would RuPaul do?'

I laughed. 'He'd probably see Mr Harris and lip sync for his dear life?'

'No, he would tell Mr Harris to sashay away.' Lizzie clicked her finger, sassy.

'I wish I could be as bold.'

I decided to keep my makeup on, just for maths. It would be a waste, after all. But mainly because I didn't want to risk being late for Mrs Powell.

Mrs Powell was one of those teachers you could tell loved her job. Her nature was free-spirited, and she loved spending her holidays at festivals or travelling through places like Thailand. She saw Cartridge High as a challenge, with it having a bad reputation. After briefly being a substitute at the school first, she had grown to love the pupils, even the more challenging ones. Lizzie affectionately nicknamed her "Honey," like the lovable teacher Miss Honey from Matilda.

'I'm not going to read your scores out loud, as that would be unkind,' Mrs Powell said as Lizzie and I took our seats in her class. 'However, there are some disappointing results, to say the least.' She handed

everyone their results individually.

Lizzie announced, 'Yes! I'm delighted with my

predicted grade.'

'I scored higher than I thought, too.' I smiled. Maths

wasn't my strongest subject, but I think I always made

more effort because it was Mrs Powell's class.

The room's noise lifted as everyone asked their

neighbour what result they had.

'Quiet, year eleven!' Mrs Powell raised her voice, and

the room went silent. She had authority and respect

down to a tee.

'Miss? I'm not sure mine is correct,' Ben Roberts

questioned.

Powell chuckled. 'You were probably talking to

Mohammed too much.' Mohammed was Ben's table

neighbour; he played on the same football team as Ben outside of school and was forever told to stop chatting by Mrs Powell.

Ben appeared concerned. 'Miss, I'm being serious. This must be a mistake.'

'Come and chat with me after class, Ben.'

Ben Roberts is tall, has short afro hair and a physique that says he doesn't ever treat himself to Krispy Kreme donuts. He's well-respected at Cartridge for his football skills, which were documented in the local newspaper, the Echo. The Echo dubbed Ben a future rising football star for Oldport and announced his team has an upcoming match that will broadcast on channel S4C. He's the type of lad that's always picked first during Physical Education, whereas I'm always chosen last, and even then, the team that gets me is annoyed. Being rejected by your peers for being rubbish at something never feels great.

'Want to come to gay pride with me?' I whispered to Lizzie.

'Are there going to be any crowds?'

'Definitely.'

'Let me think about it, okay?'

Oldport would be hosting the first-ever gay pride on the high street. I thought it would be a fun day out for Lizzie and me to go along, but since the pandemic, she seems to have developed some sort of social anxiety. Especially in crowds. Even shopping with her mum at the local Asda around a busy payday could be too much for Lizzie.

After class, Mr Harris spotted Lizzie and me walking past his office window. To his dismay, I was still wearing the makeup he demanded I remove earlier, but we were purposely walking too fast for him to catch us. Ben Roberts was also making his way past Mr Harris's office door, and Mr Harris shouted after him.

Lizzie and I were unsure if Mr Harris was on our trail, so we linked arms and dodged other pupils in the corridor as our legs and feet couldn't move fast enough to get away.

'Watch it!'

'Sorry!' I shouted back to a student we had almost knocked over.

We pushed open a side entrance door and, once outside, we leaned over and gasped for fresh air.

Lizzie promised to keep an eye out for Mr Harris as I

took my blazer off and unzipped my backpack to

squeeze it in.

'Great! Come on.' Lizzie kept tapping me anxiously.

'Is Harris coming?' I asked as I threw my bag over my

shoulder.

'No, Jackson.'

Lewis Jackson approached us and started teasing me

regarding my makeup, slyly asking if I was doing it to

attract Lewis's attention. He got right into my face, and

I could smell the cigarette he had just smoked.

Lizzie grumbled, 'Get a grip, Lewis.'

'What gay lad will fancy a boy covered in makeup?'

Lewis flicked my cheek with his fingers. He then

grabbed my bag strap so I couldn't move away from

him.

'Any money in here, then?' Lewis said as he rattled the bag's zip.

I had no control, and I had to get Lewis to back off. The timing was everything as Ben Roberts came from nowhere and tackled Lewis onto the grass.

'Leave Cory alone!' Ben said in Lewis's face.

'I was only messing around. Anyway, what is it to you, Ben?'

'What do you mean what is it to me?' Ben clenched his fist into Lewis's shirt, and Lewis took a giant gulp.

'Well, you're not exactly friends with these people.'

'Actually, I am.' Ben was lying so Lewis would back off. Lizzie and I were underdogs at this school and would never hang out with someone as cool as Ben Roberts.

Ben unlocked his fist from Lewis's shirt and stood up. Lewis walked off in a huff, picking loose bits of grass from his uniform. He knew he could never win a fight with Ben Roberts. I was thankful for the intervention from Ben.

'Wow, cheers, Ben.'

'Mr Harris has–'

'It's no worries. Say no more, Ben. I'll remove it now.'

I knew full well Mr Harris would have sent Ben to relay his message.

'Also, will you do something for me?'

'I said I'll remove my makeup.'

'Thanks, but it's not that; I'm struggling with maths, and Mrs Powell pointed out if I fail my GCSE, I won't be able to do the football academy next year.' Ben sounded concerned. Football was his everything, and if he didn't make the sixth-form football academy, many people would see it as a massive failure, so he needed

my support.

Lizzie gave me the side-eye as I tried to delegate her to

help out.

'Please tutor me, Cory. I saved your bag from that

butthead, Lewis.'

It's not I minded helping anyone with maths, but I felt

slightly socially anxious around straight boys, especially

after the incident with Lewis at the house party. I also

thought Lizzie, being more of the mathematician,

would be the better person to help Ben, but in this

instance, I felt obliged to agree.

'Yeh, sure, I will try my best to help you.'

'Cheers, Cory. I'm also sorry you must remove your

makeup; it looks lovely.'

I wasn't wearing a blusher, but I blushed at the compliment.

Before heading to my next class, I stuck to my word and washed off my makeup in the boys' toilets. I wasn't carrying any face wash in my bag, so I used the toilets' hand soap. As I pressed on the soap dispenser, I prayed the soap wouldn't break me out in spots tomorrow, knowing hand wash was full of fragrance.

After I removed all traces of my makeup, I peered at my reflection in front of me. My eyes were puffy, my skin red and my fringe wet from the warm water. I tried to be optimistic and fake a smile for the person looking right back at me, but my lips wouldn't make a move. I had been forced to wash my identity down the basin. My eyes filled with salty water, and I closed them to release the tiny waterfall. It's so unfair, I thought.

Throughout the next lesson, many thoughts ran through my head, mainly how lovely Ben had been to get Lewis back off. I was slightly nervous about helping Ben with his maths, but the more I thought about it, the more I fancied the idea – and Ben.

Plus, this would be my opportunity to prove to everyone at Cartridge that gay boys like me could have heterosexual friendships.

Lizzie usually went home for lunch, as her parents were on a tight budget. This meant lunchtime was the perfect opportunity for me to help Ben with maths revision, so we decided to meet in the school's library.

Before heading to the library, I walked past a touching memorial I thought was unusually thoughtful of Cartridge High. Mr Waters had organised for an apple tree to be planted on the school grounds as a student nicknamed 'Apple' had their life taken back last year. I didn't know Apple, but I thought it was a lovely metaphor for those who did.

I walked into the nearly empty library, and Ben had already sat at a table. The desk was littered with books people hadn't bothered to return to their shelves, so I threw some into a pile to give me room to study.

'Hey, Cory, thanks for doing this for me. Mrs Powell said I can re-sit the test, so I've got two weeks to get my head around all of this,' Ben continued. 'You removed your makeup? Your skin is beautiful. Sorry, I don't even know why I said that.'

'It's fine.' I smiled.

Two weeks of compliments from Ben? I wondered if he was struggling with any other subjects I could assist with.

I sat in silence when I wasn't explaining the coursework to Ben. What could I say? I thought to myself.

But it was Ben who spoke first. 'I don't understand why the school doesn't allow guys to wear makeup. It must be hard to be judged on the way you want to look.'

'Hey, I choose to express myself with makeup, and I can wash it off. It must be much worse for someone of colour in the football world?'

'I've been one of the lucky ones so far – don't get me wrong, racism in football very much exists, but I think it happens to be a problem for professionals in the Premier League. I think football fans can be the worst.'

'I see.'

'So I know you love makeup. What's something you dislike?'

'I hate school.'

'Why?'

'Because I don't fit in.'

'At this school, nobody does.'

I think Ben said it to make me feel less alone.

As we were revising, I noticed a phone notification from

my mum, Michelle.

> CAN U LOOK AFTER RYAN ON FRIDAY
> NIGHT? JUST BEEN INVITED TO GO
> BINGO WITH THE WORK GIRLS XXX

'Ugh,' I huffed.

'What's up?'

'Nothing – my mum wants me to care after my five-

year-old brother this Friday. He's at an age where it's a

nightmare keeping him entertained.'

Ben had such a swag stance as he swung back on his chair using his two hands as leverage. 'Let me help you babysit?' Ben asked, casually leaning back on his chair. 'What? No – plus, you'll start getting a name for yourself being associated with me.'

People would automatically think Ben was gay if they knew we spent time together outside school. I was now trying to mirror Ben's confidence as I started leaning back on my chair with bravado. Except my hands pushed away from the table and lost their grip; I fell right back with all four chair legs up in the air – thud!

'You okay?' Ben asked as he lent his hand to pull me back up from the floor.

'I haven't attempted that before.'

'I can tell.' Ben grinned.

I sat back in my seat, feeling flustered.

Ben smiled reassuringly. 'You're doing a good job getting my head around this coursework. I'm free Friday, so let me help you with babysitting.'

'But you're going to be bored in my house; I don't have a games console or anything.'

Ben explained, 'There's more to me than game consoles. Plus, I could always teach the little man some football tricks; I'm wicked with kids. I wish I had a sibling,' he added wistfully.

'Okay, thanks, it would be nice to have your company.' Inside, I was cringing at the thought of it being so awkward at my house.

On WhatsApp, Lizzie couldn't believe it when I told her Ben Roberts was going around my house on Friday. She also warned me to be extra careful, as everyone had given us a tough time since the whole kissing-Lewis-

Jackson-at-the-house-party rumour. I couldn't afford to have another negative story about a straight boy go around the school…

Friday arrived quickly. After Ben had offered to assist in caring for my brother Ryan, this week just seemed to fly by.

As we walked to my house after school, I felt insecure about my neighbourhood. I had never seen Ben's house before. Still, I could imagine Ben probably lived in a lovely suburb of Oldport – especially as Ben and his dad were the type of family to have Sky TV with all the channels and go on holiday abroad every year. In contrast, my mum could only ever afford the odd caravan holiday in West Wales. I was incredibly proud of my mum, though, as she worked hard to ensure we had everything we needed and regularly worked extra hours at her job at our local Sainsbury's supermarket to make ends meet.

The Boy In Makeup

As we walked home, I prayed my next-door neighbour Steve wouldn't be sitting outside his house drinking cans of Strongbow. Or the neighbours' cheeky kids on the other side weren't home jumping on their trampoline, as they would have shouted something immature if I walked into my house with another boy. Thankfully, the street was unusually quiet, and I led us into my semi-detached council house.

Ben first noticed my pictures of when I was little and family photos of my mum, myself, and Ryan. He also said the house had the aroma of a home that was 'homey' – but I think it was the garlic from my mum's shepherd's pie.

I took Ben's North Face jacket and hung it next to mine in the hallway, and Ben slid his shoes off before we walked upstairs.

'Do you need to pick up your little brother from school?'

'No,' I explained. 'My mum's friend Trudy will be here with him in a minute. She has a little girl the same age as Ryan, so they take turns doing the school run.'

Ben continued to compliment my home as we climbed the staircase. The compliments made me calm and less nervous showing him around. It wasn't that I was embarrassed by my house, but I knew Ben probably had a lot more than we did. Then, before I could give Ben a bedroom tour, his phone started to vibrate in his pocket, and when he peered at the screen, he seemed embarrassed to answer it in front of me. Ben dived into the bathroom to take the call, slamming the door shut behind him. His secretiveness made my mind go into turmoil. What if it's Ben's girlfriend? What if he was in a serious relationship and hadn't managed to mention it? While Ben was in the bathroom, the doorbell rang, and a larger-than-life Trudy came inside with Ryan. Trudy had been Mum's best friend since their school days and was even there in the delivery room when I was born.

'What's occurring, Cory boy?' Trudy shouted in her thick Welsh valley accent.

I ran downstairs to greet Trudy and Ryan. 'Nothing much; I've got a friend around.'

'Boy or girl?'

'Boy. Shhh,' I whispered.

'Your mum didn't tell me you've got a boyfriend now?' She smirked while placing her fists on her waist.

'He's not a boyfriend. He's a friend from school.'

Trudy cackled. 'So, where is he then? You haven't left him hiding in your wardrobe, have you?'

'He's in the bathroom upstairs on the phone.'

'So, your new fella is talking to his girlfriend, and that's why we're whispering.'

'He's not my boyfriend!'

'All right. I'd love to chat about your love life, but I've got things to do and people to see, so I'll be on my way.'

Before Trudy could leave, creaking footsteps came down the stairs. So, she decided to stay a little longer to meet my new friend.

'All right?' Trudy had a cheeky smirk on her face. She didn't know what Ben would look like, but she certainly wasn't expecting a buff footballer to come down the stairs. He was slightly taller than I was and had perfect straight white teeth, which lit up the entire room when he smiled. His arms bulged through his sleeves, and his pecks poked out of the fabric of his top... If I weren't gay, I'd still fancy Ben!

'Trudy, this is Ben, my friend from school; we're hanging out.' I was nervous, not knowing what would come out of Trudy's gob. Ryan's eyes lit up when I continued. 'He's going to teach Ryan how to do some football tricks.'

'Hi." Ben smiled.

'Listen, lovey, if you ever want me to play with your balls…'

'Out! Out! Out!' I interrupted Trudy and ushered her out of the house. I knew she was bantering with Ben, but it wasn't appropriate language for my guest, who might not appreciate her crude humour.

'Gosh, you're losing your sense of humour, Cory boy.' She laughed as she was forced out of the door.

'Nice to meet you.' Ben smiled as Trudy waved goodbye.

'She seems wild!'

'Sorry about her,' I said, pushing the front door closed.

'Don't apologise. I love people who are characters.'

Ryan lightened the room when he peeled the Velcro on
his school bag and got out a picture he had drawn of
the family with a new dog named Peppa Pig.

'I keep telling you, Ryan, it's never going to happen,' I
said, ruffling his hair and squashing little Ryan's hope
we'd be able to afford a dog.

We ventured into the kitchen. 'Shall I make us all a
drink?'

I slowly poured Sainbury's value orange squash into two
tumblers and one beaker. But there was one thing I was
itching to know. I had to ask Ben who was on the
phone.

'Ah. That was my dad.' A massive weight shifted off my shoulders. I didn't know why as we were just friends; Ben could have a girlfriend, of course.

'Silly me, I forgot to tell him I was coming over here. Sorry, I had to be rude and take the call privately.'

'Don't apologise; your dad must know where you are. I didn't know if it was your girlfriend...' The words just came out of my mouth.

'Ah, about that...' A few seconds pause from Ben. Then he announced he didn't have a girlfriend. Church bells rang inside my head as I took a swig of squash.

'Cory has boyfriends!' Ryan chimed in. I almost spat out my drink!

I swallowed the squash and took a breath. 'No, I don't, cheeky!' I tickled Ryan, smirking at Ben's response, but I made out it was because of Ryan's cheeky comment.

Ben went out into the back garden to find a football and started impressing Ryan with his tricks.

'Let me show you how to get good at dribbling,' Ben said to my brother as he did some impressive tricks with the ball.

'I don't dribble anymore as I don't have a dummy,' Ryan said, trying to sound grown up in front of Ben.

'No, not that kind of dribbling. It's where you manoeuvre the football without letting the defenders get it.' Ben dribbled the ball around some garden toys. I watched Ben as he showed off his football skills; there was no denying he's talented.

While Ben entertained Ryan, I decided to slip away and change out of my school uniform. I was hungry but too shy around him to eat, in case I got any around my mouth or down my clothes because of nerves. If a boy ever offered me on a date to go somewhere like Nando's, I'd never know how to eat my food while nervous. I'd much rather have a movie and chatter instead.

There wouldn't be enough shepherd's pie for Ben anyway, which would also be rude.

On my way towards the back garden door, laughter came from Ryan and Ben.

I stood at the doorway and peered out into the garden.

'You guys having fun?' I said, feeling more like myself now that I had changed out of my school uniform.

'Nice jumper.' It was my favourite burgundy Jack Wills jumper that I got last Christmas.

'Cheers.'

He's just being nice, Cory. Do not let the compliments go to your head and think it might be anything more.

Ryan tried to keep up with Ben, then paused to ask me what was for dinner and groaned that he was hungry, rubbing his eyes. Ryan was clearly hungry and tired. It was good timing as it had started to rain, so Ryan and Ben legged it inside, and I locked the backdoor behind us.

I tapped some buttons, made a few beeps, and microwaved some leftover shepherd's pie for Ryan.

I started making salt and vinegar crisp sandwiches for myself and Ben. It wasn't until I went into the fridge to grab some butter that I realised my mum had left some food ingredients with a note asking if I could make some cakes for Sainsbury's charity bake sale on Saturday morning.

'Oh, no way – it's tomorrow.'

I moaned to Ben that my mum was always giving me jobs to do and that I wouldn't have time to make charity cakes for her.

Although, to Mum's defence, if she were aware Ben was coming over, she probably wouldn't have asked me as she'd know it would be rude to abandon my guest by being glued to the kitchen.

'Hey, besides football, making cakes is my thing.' Ben smirked and rolled up his sleeves.

It was a surprise as Ben making cakes didn't seem like Ben's thing. I would have never imagined Ben giving Betty Crocker a run for her money, but here we were.

'It's fine – my mum will have to donate shop-bought cakes instead.'

'Your mum can't do that. Cory, if you make Ryan his dinner, I've got this. I need a large mixing bowl, a wooden spoon, and... can you set the oven to 190 degrees?' Ben started gathering the ingredients together from out of the fridge. I couldn't help but be impressed at Ben taking the lead.

I also enjoyed being entertained by Ben, now acting as if he were Jamie Oliver. He spoke in a posh English accent into the wooden spoon like it was a microphone. 'On today's show, I've got my special guest, Cory, and we're making the finest chocolate brownies.'

We were both weak at his attempt at an English accent, which sounded more Australian.

I put Ryan's food in the living room as he happily ate his dinner on a small table in front of the television, watching the CBeebies children's channel.

'Do you have an electrical whisk? Or if not, I can do it with a regular one,' Ben asked as I walked back into the kitchen. I pulled an electrical whisk out from one of the kitchen drawers and plugged it into the wall.

'As requested, sir.' I flipped the wall switch on.

Ben turned on the electrical whisk – WHOOOSH!!! And liquid chocolate cake mix immediately went all over him and the kitchen counter.

'Oh my gosh, I'm so sorry.'

I laughed. 'Why are you apologising? It's hardly gone anywhere other than over you.' I handed him some wet wipes to get it off his clothing.

'Is it all off now?' Ben glanced down at his shirt.

'You've still got it all over your face. Here, let me help you.' I grabbed a fresh wet wipe from the packet.

I wiped the mixture off Ben's cheek. At this point, Ben looked into my eyes, and I didn't realise how close I had gotten to Ben. So close I got a whiff of his cologne, which was aquatic and fresh. I felt his hands slowly move onto my waist.

We both closed our eyes. We leaned in to kiss. And then our lips touched. It was like the world had stopped for a moment, and I floated on air. I questioned myself if it actually happened or if I just imagined it.

'Mummy's home!' Ryan burst into the kitchen. Ben pushed me away quite forcefully, and we quickly dispersed. My chest felt so tight I thought my heart was going to escape.

The front door slammed shut, and I heard Mum's keys jingle in the hallway. Why is she home so early? I thought. I wasn't expecting her home until at least ten p.m., which was a standard when she went out with her friends from work.

Ryan ran up to the kitchen counter and rose up on tiptoe to appear over the worktop. 'What are you making, Cory?' he asked, while my mum shouted, 'CORY, Ryan has made a massive mess in this living room!' as she observed the state of the living room where Ryan had eaten his food.

I ignored her request and shouted back, 'Mum, come and meet my friend Ben.' I didn't know what to do with my facial expressions as I kissed Ben, and Ben pushed me away. And to top it off, Mum had come home so early.

'Oh, hiya, love – excuse the hair; it's raining heavily out there. It's a good job I drive; otherwise, I would have got stuck in all that,' Mum said, looking out the window at the weather.

'Hi, it's great to meet you.' Ben smiled.

'Nice to meet you too, love. Making some cakes for charity, are we?'

'Oh, yeh. We were. We are.' I was feeling extremely fidgety.

'Mum, you're home early?' I said as I scratched the back of my neck.

'Well, we hadn't even got to bingo as Paula had got absolutely bladdered in Spoons, and because bingo was planned for her birthday, we said we'll go next week now when she's in a better state.' Mum proceeded to laugh at the situation.

While my mum was chatting with Ben in the kitchen, I quickly vacuumed the living room floor and picked up some of the food Ryan had dropped on the sofa. How can someone so small make such a mess? I thought.

After I place the hoover back under the stairs, I entered the kitchen, and Ben announced, 'I think I better head home now as I told my dad I wouldn't stay too long.' I knew it was an excuse as Ben had planned to stay at my house much longer.

'But you haven't finished making cakes for my cake sale. Was it something I said?' Mum joked.

'No, not at all. I just realised the time.' Ben headed out to the hallway to grab his shoes.

'I'll grab my shoes, too. Mum, I'll need to start again when I'm back.'

Ben seemed flustered, and I needed to apologise to him alone.

'You can't come with me; it's chucking it down.'

'I'll drop you off, love; it's no worries. I'll grab my jacket.'

Mum made sure I turned the cooker off before we left,

and we all squeezed into my mum's small blue Nissan.

On the way to Ben's, my rumbling stomach returned

because I had crossed the line by kissing Ben. What was

I thinking? What if he told everyone in school? My

chest had palpitations. I didn't want my life to get even

worse at school. It was already unbearable as it was, and

that was just a rumour; this time it was the truth.

'So, how do you know Cory?' My mum attempted to

make small chitchat en route.

'He's been helping me with my maths coursework.'

'Really? I didn't realise my son was such a brain box.'

Usually, I'd say something sarcastic back to my mum,

like I clearly got my intelligence from my father, but I

just sat in silence. I couldn't concentrate on any of the

conversations going back and forth. I just stared out at the window, deep in my thoughts.

'This is my street.' Ben looked out the window and pointed. 'This house by there is mine.'

The street was precisely how I imagined it to be: big four-bedroom detached houses with long drives, multiple cars, and integrated garages. This was the nice side of Oldport that had only been built a few years prior.

'Oh, now this is posh! Nice to meet you.' Mum waved as Ben climbed out of the car.

'Bye, thanks for the lift. See you on Monday in school, Cory.'

I couldn't say anything. I froze as Ben held the door open and waited for my response.

'Cory, aren't you going to say goodbye to Ben?'

'Sorry see you, Ben,' I said, snapping out of my daydream or, should I say, living nightmare.

Ben closed the car door, and Mum drove off.

'Everything all right, love? You seem like you're in your own world,' Mum said, appearing in the rearview mirror. She flipped the car's indicator on to turn right, and the clicking noise was as if I was on a game show and I didn't know the answer to the million-pound question. Click. Click. Click.

'Cory?'

'Yeh, fine, Mum.'

I kept typing up an apology WhatsApp message to Ben but then erased it as nothing sounded right.

Sorry about the kiss – Delete.

Sorry for kissing you – Delete.

Sorry – Delete.

The journey home flew by as I tried to type up a message. I hadn't even realised we pulled outside my house until my mum came around to unbuckle Ryan. I unfastened my seat belt, my attention fixed entirely on my phone. As I got out, I stupidly tripped over a paving slab. I didn't hurt myself, but my phone spun into the air. 'Nooo!' I squealed.

As it hit the ground, it sounded like someone had smashed a tiny bottle of wine.

My phone faced the ground. As I picked it up, time was in slow motion, and I prayed it was not broken despite the dramatic sound effect. I turned the device around, and the screen was entirely unusable. The once Ariana Grande wallpaper on my lock screen was now psychedelic and unrecognisable.

'Mind the glass on your hands!' Mum shouted as I continued to tap the cracked screen as if it would just start to work magically.

'Please work. You can't die on me.' I proceeded to tap my phone's screen, but still nothing.

My whole life was on that phone – TikTok, Instagram, the world outside Oldport, diversity, Spotify, and Ben.

'Oh no!' I covered my mouth with my palm as the realisation hit me – I didn't even get to apologise to Ben! Tears streamed down my face, and I wasn't quite sure what hyperventilating was, but I was probably doing that right now. Ben would be busy with football practice all weekend, and I would have to wait until Monday to apologise.

Hundreds of anxious thoughts ran around my mind. I didn't want to feel like this, but it was as if I were falling down a well, and my hands couldn't grip the sides as I fell. Stay calm and think rationally, I kept reminding myself.

'Aww, don't be upset.' My mum side-hugged me with one arm while the other held Ryan. She didn't know what was happening, why I was really upset, but presumed I was this sad because I had just broken my phone. But really I was wondering how would I apologise to Ben now?

It was Monday morning, and Lewis was walking

towards me down the corridor at school.

'Cory and Ben up in the tree, K-I-S-S-I-N-G.'

'What?'

'You heard me,' Lewis said, poking his tongue out as I

walked past him. He stank as if he had just drank ten

energy drinks, but that was the least of my worries.

Ben told everyone at school that I kissed him. I felt

dizzy as the hallway spun around me.

And to make matters even worse, the intercom then

announced, 'Cory James is to report to the headmaster's

office immediately.'

The school hall erupted, and my peers shouted childish

comments like 'Ohh, what have you done?' and

'Naughty boy'. I wasn't sure if it was because I was

being called to the headmaster's office or if they were

mocking me for kissing Ben.

I smiled awkwardly, trying to show that they didn't

bother me.

Walking alone down the hallway, it was as if my feet

didn't want to carry me, and the distance to the

headmaster's office had never felt this long.

Why was I being called in? Ben might have complained

that I kissed him on Friday afternoon. I searched

everywhere for him this morning to apologise, but it

seemed like a waste of time, as he'd already told

everyone. Including the headmaster? No, that didn't

seem right.

Mr Waters wouldn't care about me kissing Ben.

I took a big gulp; I remembered how Mr Harris had

warned me that if I carried on wearing makeup to

school, he would contact my mother and get her permission to put me in a dress. Of course, Michelle would never agree to Mr Harris's bullying tactics, but I had a bad feeling that I could be humiliated in front of the school by being made to wear a frilly dress, and everyone would laugh at me. My heart pounded as if I was the one who had drunk ten energy drinks.

I knocked on the headmaster's office door, and a friendly voice invited me in. The headmaster, Mr Waters, and a lady I hadn't seen before were both sat down, and their faces appeared sympathetic.

'Come on in, Cory, and shut the door behind you,' the friendly lady said. I sat down opposite them both and placed my bag on the floor.

'I'm Miss Pearce; I'm going to take notes during this conversation for Mr Waters. I'm from a different school, so I'm here as an unbiased observer. Mr Waters will

explain what this is all about anyway.'

I was puzzled.

'Cory, it's been brought to the school's attention that Mr

Harris has been unkind towards you. The complaint

has come from another teacher at the school, and the

allegations are quite serious,' Mr Waters said.

I listened to what they had to say as they read out dates

and times when a staff member at Cartridge had

overheard comments from Mr Harris towards me,

mainly regarding wearing makeup. Mr Harris sounded

more shocking when read out loud in text.

'Now, we've already made the tough decision to suspend

Mr Harris from his role here at Cartridge.'

I was gobsmacked. Sure, I didn't like Mr Harris, but I

would have never wanted anyone to risk losing their job.

'We want to check that these comments made towards you are correct and that you'd like to support this complaint with your signature,' Mr Waters said.

'If I say it's true, what would happen to Mr Harris?'

Miss Pearce explained, 'Cory, if all this is true, then Mr Harris will, rightly so, be dismissed from his role at Cartridge High. But you mustn't worry about this – you will be protected.'

'Well, it's not true.'

Both teachers were surprised.

'Cory, I can tell this may be difficult for you, but people who say things like this need to be held accountable for their actions. You could also be helping future students who might not be as strong as you avoid future conflicts with Mr Harris,' Mr Waters added.

'No, I'm sorry; I can't.'

'You don't need to make a decision now. We will still need to investigate Mr Harris, and he's already been made fully aware of the complaint made against him,' explained Mr Waters.

I felt dreadful as someone could potentially lose their job because of me. The school's policy was that I shouldn't wear makeup, and now Mr Harris was in trouble. I was in the wrong.

'Am I free to leave now?' I wanted to get out of the office.

'Yes. Please remember my office is always open. I want Cartridge to be a place where everyone can be themselves,' said Mr Waters.

Where everyone can be themselves? What about boys in makeup? I thought.

'Is there anything else you'd like to say before you go, Cory?' Miss Pearce asked.

'Well, I am a boy who likes wearing makeup. I don't want to be a girl; I want to express myself. Walking down the hallway, you will see many girls and female teachers wearing makeup because they want to feel empowered. Girls are allowed to cut their hair short and wear school trousers. But for some reason, with our school policy, it's not okay for boys to wear makeup. It's exclusive.'

'I see. I suppose we allow all kinds of wacky hair colours to express ourselves; makeup can be a lot tamer. I'm on a Zoom call with my boss later today. I'll see what I can do, Cory. Leave it with me.' Mr Waters smiled and seemed upbeat about the idea.

During break time, I saw Lizzie sitting at our usual bench. I knew I looked guilty as I walked up to her, as that's precisely how I felt. I wanted to tell her that I was very sorry that everyone would give us an even tougher time now that I had actually kissed a straight boy. But before I could apologise, she asked me what happened in Mr Waters's office. The fact that Mr Harris had been suspended avoided my having to talk about the kiss. As I explained the complaint against Mr Harris, I wondered if Lizzie knew anything about the Ben kiss, as that would have typically been at the top of her list of conversations as it would impact both of us. Lizzie couldn't understand why I hadn't told the truth and exposed Mr Harris; he had given me such a bad school experience for a while and deserved to be held accountable. I still needed to tell Lizzie about kissing

Ben, so I started explaining what had happened, and then Ben walked up to us.

'Cory, can I speak to you for a second?'

We walked alongside each other in silence until we were safe to talk without anyone hearing our conversation. Ben seemed annoyed, and I had never seen him look serious before. As much as I was angry at him for telling everyone about our kiss, I secretly thought that being mad at me suited him.

'What were you going to tell Lizzie just then?'

'How you've told everyone I kissed you,' I snapped.

Ben's eyes widened. 'What?'

'Lewis Jackson knows I kissed you.'

'How?' Ben raised one eyebrow.

I explained what Lewis had said, and I was confused as to why Ben started chuckling to himself.

'Cory, that's Lewis teasing you because I got him to back off. You're being paranoid; I haven't mentioned anything to anyone, and I'd appreciate it if you didn't.' The way he said the last bit had a bit of an edge to it.

'I'm sorry. I'm also sorry for kissing you.' I spoke softly.

'It's fine, just don't tell anyone, okay?'

That was more than fine by me.

'Also, why have you ghosted me?' That also sounded like it had an edge.

Shit, I hadn't told Ben that my phone was smashed. He must have thought I was ignoring him over the weekend.

'I dropped my phone. I didn't ghost you.'

Ben showed off his million-pound smile for the first time today. 'You didn't?'

I explained how I had dropped my phone outside my house after we dropped him off and that I had just spent my whole birthday and Christmas savings on ordering another one, which was an older model than the previous one, but it'd do for now.

We both laughed about our paranoia as we headed back over to Lizzie.

'You really thought I ghosted you, huh?' I side-smirked.

Ben shoved me. 'Shut up.'

The three of us sat on the bench, and I explained the complaint against Mr Harris. Ben sided with Lizzie that I should have been upfront, but he respected my decision. The three of us tried to think of which teacher was the whistle-blower. I thought about the dates and times when the incidents occurred and which teacher was around; it had to be Mrs Honey, aka Mrs Powell.

I wanted to find out, and because we had a great relationship with Mrs Powell, we knew we could go and ask her.

Luckily, we caught Mrs Powell before she left her classroom for lunch. When I explained the complaint, Mrs Powell was sad to hear that I had experienced that in school with Mr Harris.

'I wish you had come to me and told me, Cory, this is not okay. So no, it wasn't me who told the school about Mr Harris, as I wasn't aware. Plus, if I had heard anything, I wouldn't make a formal complaint like this without your consent first.' Mrs Powell, being professional, acted as if we were the first to tell her, but something told me that the teachers were probably all briefed about Mr Harris's suspension by Mr Waters.

'We have no idea who could have told the school about this,' said Lizzie.

'Well, someone is looking out for you kids, thank god!' We didn't want to keep Mrs Powell too long as this was her break time, so the three of us stood up to exit.

Before we went, Mrs Powell added, 'Ben, I'm sure you won't mind me mentioning this in front of the others, but your coursework is rapidly improving. Whatever you're doing, keep it up!'

'Thanks!' Ben beamed as we opened her classroom door to leave.

'Oh, and before you go, Cory.'

'Yes, Mrs?'

'Next time something like that happens, make sure you hold that person accountable for their actions.'

'Will do.'

Before the end of the school day, Mr Waters approached me to double-check I wasn't going to follow through with the grievance. I confidently declined as I would have a guilty conscious if Mr Harris were let go because of me. Although I didn't sign off on the complaint, there was still a chance that Mr Harris could be sacked.

Mr Waters informed me that I was now allowed to wear makeup to school, like any female who went to Cartridge High. I thought I would be happy and pretended I was, but deep down, I felt so responsible for the situation with Mr Harris.

Mr Waters not only lifted the ban on boys being allowed to wear makeup, but he also appointed me as the school's new LGBTQ+ ambassador. I cringed at the thought when he asked if I was happy to accept the role, but I didn't want to be negative after he changed the no-makeup policy, so I just nodded in acceptance. It was Mr Waters's boss's idea as he wanted to make the school more inclusive. My assigned project would ensure that the school actively supported all LGBTQ+ pupils without discrimination – which, I guessed, was quite cool!

It was Friday, and I was on the lunch break bench with Ben and Lizzie.

Ben informed me that his club had cancelled football practice for tomorrow. And, because it was forecast to be a hot day, he asked me if I fancied riding our bikes to the park and hanging out instead.

Lizzie sat on the other side of Ben. While he was asking, she waved her hands and mimed the words 'No way.'

I thought about it for a second. Could I really hang out with Ben again outside of school when the last time I kissed him and almost ruined our friendship?

'Sure, would love to!'

'Cool.' Ben smiled.

Lizzie rolled her eyes in the background. Of course I was going to agree to hang out with Ben. Lizzie was concerned that nothing good would come out of our unlikely friendship, and she would be even worse if she knew I had planted one on Ben. But it's perfectly normal for me to have a straight friend, even if we didn't have much in common. Plus, I enjoyed being in Ben's company.

One simple rule going forward: I just needed to avoid trying to kiss him!

Saturday was here, and I was chilling at the park with Ben.

'Take your socks off and feel the grass on your toes; it's a weird feeling,' I said, standing on the freshly cut grass.

'You're funny. It's not like this is the beach. People don't take their socks off at the park, Cory.' Ben laughed.

'Honestly, try it. It's satisfying.' I smiled back.

'Okay, if you insist.'

Ben threw his socks off, tiptoed around the red tartan picnic blanket and avoided stepping on any beige picky food.

'What do you think?' I asked once Ben's feet nested onto the grass.

Ben's hands were on his hips. 'Yeh, it does feel good. How is it so refreshing?'

I paused to answer. 'Probably... dog pee?'

Ben cringed. 'Na, mate!' He couldn't chuck his Adidas socks back on fast enough.

The park was typically busy for a hot day. There were dogs barking and radio music playing on mobile phones in the background. Despite signage forbidding any fires or barbecues, a group of teenagers slightly older than us had a barbecue on the field, which smelt delicious.

Ben was lying down with his legs arched, his backpack under his head, engrossed in watching a football match clip on YouTube.

I noticed a family with small children had set up a tent for shade.

'The family over there have brought a little tent to the park. That's really cute,' I observed.

'Perhaps it's for them to have some shade if they couldn't find a tree?' Ben appeared over his phone.

'I used to love camping when I was younger,' I admitted.

'Why don't we do it, then? It could be fun.'

'Go camping?'

Ben sat up and slid his phone into his pocket. 'Yes, why not? I have all the gear at my house; my dad and I used to do it quite frequently,' Ben reminisced.

'My mum won't agree to it if there are no adults.' The truth is my mum won't let boys stay over in my room, so she's never going to agree to slumbering in a tent with Ben, even though he's straight.

'I would love to show you this place my dad and I used to visit.'

'Unless… I suppose it could work?' I spoke out loud as I thought up a plan.

'What you thinking?'

'Well, I could say Lizzie is camping with her parents, and they've asked me along.'

'Argh, I don't know if we should lie to your mum, Cory.' Ben was being his usual sensible self.

'It'll be fine, and she won't find out as she doesn't have Lizzie's family on Facebook.'

'It's worth a try, I guess.'

Later, Ben went to his house to dig out his old camping equipment and got permission from his father to go camping with friends. Meanwhile, I told a compelling story to my mum how Lizzie's parents had invited me to go camping. She also agreed to let me stay out for the night and gave me money for food as she didn't want Lizzie's parents to put their hands in their pockets.

We rode our bikes and met at a petrol station that wasn't too far away from the campsite to grab snacks and food for our barbecue later.

When we walked into the petrol station, the door made a ding-dong noise, and we were clocked by a grumpy shop assistant almost immediately. We were the only customers in the shop, which wasn't unusual for a warm Saturday afternoon as everyone was probably sitting in beer gardens or having garden parties. My hand instantly froze as I picked up an ice-cold soda can from a fridge and ventured farther to find some goodies.

The grumpy middle-aged man stood at the end of the aisle, watching us as we browsed disposable barbecues. I could sense the shop assistant's beady eyes staring at us, making me uncomfortable.

'Is everything all right?' I nervously smiled at the man.

Ben was now aware we were being watched.

'Just making sure you boys will be purchasing today,' the man said in a huff.

'Right. Well, we're not going to steal anything.'

Ben kept his head to the floor, having never been to this store before and wondering if this was the normal level of customer service. I had been many times before and was never interrogated like this.

'I'm sure you're not going to steal anything, but so you know, boys, I've got CCTV,' the man said in a passive-aggressive tone as he made his way back behind the till.

'Do you think he thinks we're someone else?' I whispered to Ben.

But Ben didn't respond. Then something clicked inside my head.

'Ah, Ben, do you think this might be because you're Black?' I whispered.

'I'm not sure.' Ben chewed on his fingernails. It must be something he does when he's anxious.

'Right!' I snapped. 'I'm not having this.' I grabbed the last item we needed – a pack of giant marshmallows – and marched straight to the till. What Mrs Powell said about holding someone accountable for their actions resonated in my head.

'Cory.' Ben grabbed my arm. 'Don't, it's fine! Honest,' he whispered.

The man sat behind a counter sea of confectionary, which consisted of a wide range of colourful chocolate and chewing gums. He started to scan the items, taking no care and throwing them into a carrier bag.

'Does John ever visit this branch?' I asked the sour-faced man. Ben was trying to think who John was.

'John, who?'

'Wow, you don't know who John is; he's only the area director of Star petrol stations. Does he ever visit?'

The man asked, intrigued, 'I don't think he ever has. How do you know our area director?'

'He's my dad, who claims to always be at this petrol station working most nights. My mum sent me in today to find out if her suspicions of him having an affair are true,' I explained confidently.

The man was speechless. 'Oh.'

'Don't worry. I won't tell my dad you told me.'

'Honestly, I– I didn't…' the man stuttered.

'But then I might mention that you were watching us and accusing us of potentially stealing.'

'I– I didn't mean…' The man attempted to backtrack.

'I want you to apologise to my friend,' I said sternly.

'Cory, it's fine.'

'I-I'm sorry. This is all one big misunderstanding. I can assure you, sir,' the man said as he handed over the shopping bag.

As soon as we got outside, Ben huffed and grabbed his bike.

'What did I do?' I shouted over Ben as he started peddling.

'Ben, wait! I'm sorry if I embarrassed you?'

Ben placed his foot on the ground to stop his bike.

'Did I upset you?'

'Cory, I asked you not to do anything.'

'I'm sorry, I was trying to punish the man for judging us.'

'You said you thought he was being racist,' Ben said.

'I was suspicious, yes.'

'Well, I asked you not to do anything, but you had to save me.'

'I didn't like it, so I wanted to stick up for you.'

'You're a good person, Cory, but I need to show you something.'

We rode our bikes to a nearby bus stop and sat on the attached bench. Ben loaded YouTube and handed me his phone.

'Watch this,' he said as he turned up the volume.

The video title was 'The white saviour trope explained'.

The video educated me on how a 'white saviour' is a white person who rescues a non-white person or group

from conflict and struggle, hailing themselves as a hero.
Seeing the examples of movies that depict a white
saviour, I realised my action was problematic, and I
should have respected Ben when he asked me to stop.

'I didn't mean to offend you, Ben.'

'I know you didn't mean to, but I hope you can see now
why it frustrated me. I don't need to be saved.'

'I get it now. I'm not educated on racial injustices, but I
want to learn.'

Ben opened his arms to hug me.

'I feel bad,' I said as my friend hugged me.

When Ben finished hugging me, he kissed my cheek.

'Stop worrying.'

It worked because now all I could think of was being
kissed on the cheek. Also, Ben was brave to peck me on
my cheek at a bus stop, as anyone could have seen it

while driving past, especially if they were from our school. He's so in touch with his sexuality that he's not bothered about being affectionate like that with a gay friend.

Ben picked up his bike, and I climbed over mine to pick it up.

'So is John your dad?' Ben asked.

'No, I can't say I know anyone called John.'

Ben chuckled and shook his head as we rode off. I was glad we could now laugh about the situation.

It took us approximately twenty minutes to ride to the camping park. Anglers had their rods set up over the lake water, and there were table benches with families having picnics. The whole place looked like something from a postcard. It was picturesque, with high pine trees, a crystal blue lake, and little cabins, which, during colder months, I envisioned would have smoke coming from the tops.

We found a spot for the tent that wasn't too close to anyone else's. I tried to help Ben pitch the tent, but I was hopeless.

'Cory, let me set up the tent.' Ben could tell I was struggling.

'I would be useless just watching you, though.'

'Good view, isn't it?'

I nervously laughed as I wasn't sure if he meant himself or the beautiful view from where we were setting up. However, I secretly agreed as I liked Ben's arm muscles ripping through his short T-shirt sleeves. And he was even more handsome when he was trying to concentrate.

One day I hoped I could find a boyfriend as beautiful as Ben. It was like he was superhuman without any flaws at all.

'Other than fish, do you think there is any other wildlife here?'

'Like what?'

'You know… like foxes or wolves,' I carried on, biting my bottom lip.

'There are no wolves around here, but maybe the odd fox or stray dog.' Ben paused as he continued to fix up the tent. 'Why, are you scared we will get attacked at night?'

'I'm only asking.'

'I'll protect you, don't you worry.'

'I don't need saving,' I said sarcastically, in a lower voice like Ben's.

Ben threw a twig at me.

After Ben set up the tent, we had some fun on a paddle boat and then went for a scenic walk around the lake. The evening went smoothly until it was time to light the disposable barbecue to cook dinner. A friendly fisherman could tell we were struggling to light it up and walked over, offering some assistance. Ben had popped into the tent to grab another lighter when my mum's colleague Paula walked past with her dog and said hello to me. Many people walked past with their dogs as it seemed like an ideal place to go for a Saturday evening walk.

'Will this one work?' Ben asked, coming out of the tent and handing it over to the fisherman.

In a thick Bristolian accent, the guy shook the lighter and announced, 'Ah, a lot better. This lighter actually has gas inside it.' And he managed to get the barbecue going.

'Wow, cheers!'

'No worries at all; if I hadn't had my dinner already, I would have had a burger off you,' joked the friendly fisherman.

'Thanks, mate,' Ben said.

I wasn't wearing much makeup as it was the warm summertime. Still, I did have a little mascara, tinted moisturiser and bronzer on. Before the man walked away, he pointed at Ben and said, 'You can feed your girlfriend now. Enjoy!' He took his bucket hat off and then put it back on again.

Once he was out of sight, we both laughed at how he mistook me for a girl.

After our food and as the night became dark, we huddled around a small campfire.

'You're freezing.' Ben grabbed my hand to check my cold temperature.

'Didn't think I'd need a jacket tonight as it's been boiling, and we have the fire. I'll be fine.'

'Here, have this.' Ben took his hooded jumper off.

'Are you sure you're not going to be cold yourself?' I asked as Ben slipped the mustard-coloured oversized hoodie over my head.

'I brought one to wear tomorrow. I'll grab it if I get too cold. Plus, the colour suits you.' It was adorable how much Ben looked after me.

'Cheers.' I smiled. 'Gosh, I might go up in flames with the amount of cologne you've got on here. It's lush,' I said as I sniffed the hoodie.

'I sprayed my dad's Sauvage cologne,' Ben explained.

'It's masculine. I love it.'

'Thanks. I'll let Trevor know you like how he smells,' he joked.

Ben's confidence seemed to shift, and he started to act nervous.

'Cory, I want to tell you something.' His face looked worried, and he was fidgeting with his hands.

'Okay?' I whispered.

'Um. Sorry, I'm being ridiculous.' Ben laughed nervously.

'What's wrong?'

Then he paused to think about it.

'Ah, it's nothing; forget it. Honestly, it was nothing,' Ben tried to reassure me.

As the crickets were clicking and the moon was full, we put water over the fire and went to jump into our sleeping bags. Then it dawned on me that I hadn't just forgotten any warmer clothing but didn't think to pack anything to sleep in either. It was official! I was the Guinness World Record holder for the worse packer in history.

Ben nested in his sleeping bag as I stood up and rumbled around my belongings to find anything to keep me warm.

'I'll just sleep in my clothing on the floor,' I said, giving up.

'You could –' Ben paused.

'Could what?'

'I mean, there's plenty of room in here.' Ben shrugged.

I ignored Ben's offer. 'I could ask the other tents if they have a spare?'

Ben crinkled up his face. 'I wouldn't want to sleep in any stranger's bedding.'

'True,' I huffed.

It's not that I didn't want to get in the sleeping bag with Ben; I didn't want him to think I had done it on purpose or that I wasn't thinking of any other options.

Ben unzipped the sleeping bag and held it open. 'Plenty of room in here?'

My pulse was racing, and I was out of excuses, so I climbed into the sleeping bag with Ben. There wasn't much room inside, so our bodies naturally brushed against each other.

Ben joked, 'Make sure you keep your hands to yourself.'

I zipped up the sleeping bag. I was shivering, and not because it was cold. It was late, and we soon fell asleep. It became freezing within an hour of sleeping in the tent, which was so typical of Welsh weather. My body was warm, but my face was completely frozen. I was sleeping in a different direction from Ben, and I woke up to him wrapping himself around me. Ben was the big spoon with his arm holding my chest. I didn't make a move because I didn't want Ben to wake up or be embarrassed or stop what he was doing. My heart was racing fast, a mixture of nerves and excitement. I even wondered if my pulse racing so loudly could wake him up. I had never been cuddled by another boy before. What if anyone came into our tent and caught Ben spooned into me, sharing a sleeping bag? Even though it was innocent, it definitely wouldn't look that way to other people.

It took me a while to fall back asleep as my mind couldn't rest, but I finally nodded off, feeling safe with Ben's arm around me.

A noise rustled outside the tent during the early hours of Sunday morning, and it was loud enough to wake us both up.

Ben quickly moved his arm off me, which I took as a sign that he didn't realise he was doing it.

I whispered to Ben and asked if he heard the noise too, and then flashlights beamed over the polyester fabric of the tent. I wondered what was going on, and Ben started forward to investigate.

First, a voice came from the fisherman we had met the night before. Then we recognised another familiar voice. It was Michelle, my mum.

'Boys?' called my mum as Ben quickly unzipped the tent. There were two figures right in front of him. Now my heart was officially beating in overdrive.

'Mum, what are you doing here?'

'Never mind that. Pack your stuff, boys. This trip is over! I'll be waiting in my car.' My mum walked off in her dressing gown and bed hair.

'You shouldn't be fibbing about where you are, lads,' said the fisherman. We were so shocked my mum was there we didn't realise the man had got my gender right this time. Apparently, before finding our tent, my mum had stopped by the angler's tent first, asking if he had seen two boys who looked like us, and then the man realised we weren't a straight couple after all.

The friendly man helped us quietly dismantle the tent and gather our belongings into the car before we set off. Michelle gave a long yawn and drove off with me, Ben and my brother, Ryan, who was fast asleep in the back. My mum was silent most of the journey home, except for the odd yawn. As she drove us home, streetlights and shop signs lit our faces as we gazed out either side of the car windows.

Trying her best not to wake little Ryan, Mum whispered, 'Can I ask why I have been lied to?'

I cleared my throat. 'Sorry, Mum,' I said softly.

'You don't realise how worried I was; I woke up and checked my phone to glance at a Facebook notification.

Paula messaged to say you were camping alone with a much older gentleman. My mind went into overdrive.'

I don't know how my mum jumped to that conclusion when it could have been Lizzie's dad, but I know she worries about me meeting strangers on the internet.

'Oh, I see; that's a misunderstanding. It was the friendly man back there; he was helping us start our barbecue while Ben was inside the tent.'

'I had a feeling I had been lied to, so I came out to find you. I was glad it was Ben in your tent and not some random old man.'

'I'm sorry I lied.'

'Ben, you can stay on the sofa tonight; there's no point waking your father. But Cory, so you know, you're grounded.'

I said that I understood as Mum's car pulled up to the house, and once inside, she put Ryan to bed and grabbed an oversized duvet from the airing cupboard for Ben to sleep with on the sofa. I got into my bed, and even though I was comfortable camping in the tent, there's nothing quite like the comfort of your own bed. My house was much warmer, too. Despite this, I refused to take off Ben's mustard-coloured hoodie he had lent me. It smells so good, I thought. I smiled as the scent reminded me of Ben, but my smile soon disappeared when I remembered Ben explaining it was Trevor's fragrance.

Ding-dong!

Waiting on a new pencil case, I walked down the stairs to check if it was my parcel. Mum wouldn't usually let me order anything if I'm grounded, but she agreed after Ryan drew all over my old one.

My mum still blamed me and said she'd bin all my felt pens if I didn't lock them away until he's a bit older, as it would be her beautiful walls next.

Mum hummed, "Ding-dong, did somebody say Just Eat?' as she got to the front door before me.

As I got to the bottom of the stairs, Michelle held the door open, and Ben stood outside, smiling and holding a cake box. I was surprised to see Ben as he knew I was still grounded for a few more days, and he also knew my mum wouldn't allow him to come over.

'I thought you had football practice today?' I said,

looking surprised to see Ben.

'Cory, have you forgotten you're grounded until Friday?'

Michelle folded her arms.

'No, Mum.'

'Sorry, it's all my fault. My football practice got

cancelled again. I made a cake yesterday, and it's too

much for me to eat on my own, so I thought I would

bring it over. No worries, I can go home.'

'No, come on in,' Michelle said. As Ben walked in, she

glanced at the box to see if there would also be enough

for her, too.

Using my puppy dog face, I asked, 'Am I still

grounded?'

Michelle's eyes rolled, and she threw her arms into the

air. 'I'm way too soft with you boys.'

'Thanks, Mum! Are you sure?'

'Yes, but don't sneak out again. And you're on dishes and ironing duties all week.'

'Deal!'

Ben walked into the hallway and slid his shoes off.

'Come on up,' I said, excited both that I was no longer grounded and to see Ben. Ben hadn't been in my room yet, and once inside, the first thing he noticed was how much of a mess it was!

'Wow, you're a messy person!' Ben shook his head as he looked around the room, full of jumbled clothes and accessories scattered everywhere. Shamelessly, there was even an empty plate on my bedside table from this morning.

'To be fair, I didn't know you were coming.' I shrugged.

He grabbed a pair of trousers off the bed and flung them to the side.

'Well, I've got something to confess,' Ben said as he plopped himself on my bed.

'What is it?'

Ben spoke superfast. 'I lied about football practice. They didn't cancel it, I just didn't go; I'd much rather hang out with you. Plus, I thought you might like carrot cake, so I made it for us.' Ben held out the cake, but I didn't accept it.

'Wait, did you skip it when we went to the park too?' I asked.

'No, that was genuine. I just can't face football today.' Ben seemed to have a lot going on in his head. It was the same look he had when he tried to tell me something while camping.

He added, 'The thing I admire about you is you're so free.'

'Free?'

'Football isn't my passion; I do it to keep Trevor happy. It makes it harder that he's our football coach, too.'

'But you enjoy football?'

'I mean, I don't mind it, I'm a decent player, but it's too much pressure all the time. I'm not passionate about it like you are with makeup.'

'You're excellent at football, but I can help you find your passion.'

'Like what?' Ben grinned cheekily. 'Are you going to put makeup on me?'

At first, I thought he was joking, but then I realised he was serious.

'Yeh, if you want?'

'You cannot tell anyone at school.'

'Fine!'

After eating a slice of the cake, I dug deep into my makeup bag to find something I could use to make Ben pretty.

'Sit here,' I said as I pulled out my desk chair for Ben to sit on.

I applied eyes first, starting with glittery eyeshadow and dramatic mascara, then applied bright pink blusher. I only had foundation shades to match my skin tone, and as Ben's skin was darker, I skipped that part. We laughed throughout the makeover as Ben couldn't believe how over-the-top I was making him look. The final thing to apply was lip gloss.

Ben looked at my lips. 'Have you got lip gloss on now?'

'Yeh, it's a clear one, but I want to find a juicy red one for you, though.' I said, rummaging through my makeup bag.

'I've always wanted to know what lip gloss feels like.'

I picked up a lip gloss and held it up to see if it would be an ideal shade. 'Well, you'll soon find out,' I answered Ben.

'I said I want to feel the one on your lips.'

'Oh, really? Let me see if I can find it.' I scattered through my cosmetics.

'No. You don't understand.' Ben pulled my face from looking for the lip gloss and got closer. 'I want that one on your lips.'

And here it came – chocolate cake mixture on the face, part two. I looked at Ben, and he was looking back at me.

Our lips locked. Six seconds felt like a millisecond, and I knew I would be replaying this moment in my head for days. But then I panicked as I remembered how much I regretted kissing Ben the last time.

I pulled away. 'I'm so sorry.' I was scared of how Ben would react. 'That was wrong of me.' My heart was pounding so fast I thought it would escape my chest.

'Chill,' whispered Ben.

'I've kissed you again, which was wrong of me.' I placed my hand on my forehead. What had I done?

'I better kiss you back, so we're on equal grounds, then.' And Ben came towards me to kiss me again. It felt even better than it did before.

I could tell Ben was enjoying making out as he kept smiling at me, and he was a great kisser as he had big soft lips. I felt butterflies in my stomach and had feelings I'd never felt before.

While Ben and I were kissing, his phone started to ring. He pulled out his phone and glanced at the screen. It was his dad.

'I'm not answering. He's going to kick off because I missed football practice.'

Ben paused, and it was as if he realised what we had just done. 'Um, it's best we keep this a secret?'

I was disappointed and disheartened, and I think my face told Ben I was. 'Yeh, of course.' I said, forcing a smile.

I was gutted because I had been used by other straight boys who were curious before, and maybe this was Ben's motive the whole time. Ben wasn't gay, and the fact I really liked him was going to hurt me in the long run.

'It's probably a good idea for me to wash the makeup off before I go.' Ben smiled. 'Anyway, I need some more of your lip gloss.' He leaned in to kiss me again, pressing me against my bedroom door, but I pushed his chest away.

'Wait. Are you straight?' Seeing him be with a girl I could never compete with would destroy me.

'Who said I liked girls?'

A smile spread across my face.

Ben wasn't straight, and there was a chance he might also like me. Whatever stars were aligned today can spin around and do it again tomorrow or every day.

Ben explained, 'But I'm not ready to be out to anyone, not just yet. And this is why I don't think football is the right career for me; I could never be a Black footballer and openly gay, too.'

When I was helping Ben in the library, he said he had never experienced racism as a footballer, but it seemed like it's still in the back of his mind if he was to become a professional.

'You're more powerful than you think, Ben.'

'Supporters would never allow it. A Premier League Black footballer came out, Justin Fashanu, and he had loads of abuse.'

'Really? When did this happen?'

'Early nineties.'

I rolled my eyes and smirked. 'A lot has changed since the nineties, Ben. That's before we were even born.'

But Ben looked serious. 'I can't imagine my life being easy, being out. The World Cup was held in Qatar last year, where it's illegal to be homosexual. Imagine the backlash I would face if I were on the Welsh team.'

I didn't know if I was naive or optimistic, but if anyone could change the world, it's Ben.

I pointed out Mr Harris had given me a hard time wearing makeup, but I helped change the school policy. I also explained I had spoken to Mr Waters earlier today about possibly getting the school involved in the first gay pride for Oldport. As Elle Woods once said, 'Don't fight the fabric. Change it'. Ben wasn't ready to come out, which was fine with me. I couldn't believe Ben was secretly gay. I had presumed he might be straight or, at a stretch, bisexual. My gaydar was officially broken. But the best thing of all: he said he likes me. I felt like I won the lottery or the biggest makeup giveaway on Instagram. There's a bounce in my step as I walked around my room and felt euphoric.

Ben texted his dad, which meant he couldn't stay much longer as football practice had already finished. His dad would be on his way to collect him. He was already in trouble for skipping today, so I helped him wash off the makeover. Trevor would not be pleased to see Ben in makeup; being grounded for life would probably be his punishment. I handed Ben my Clinique cleanser, and soon the makeup swirled around the sinkhole, a rainbow mishmash of different colours swimming around the water as he cleansed his face. Ben gave me another kiss before we went downstairs. This time, his face smelt fresh from the soap.

I didn't want him to go. Now we'd started, I didn't want us to stop kissing each other.

'Please don't mention any of this to anyone.'

I grabbed his hand and looked directly into his eyes. 'I

won't.'

I took GCSE Art mainly because it's theoretical, and many makeup techniques came from art. If I were better at being an artist, that would hopefully transition into becoming better at makeup. The other art students, except Lizzie, took it because it seemed more fun than studying something like science.

Just before class, Lizzie went to the toilet, and Ben was arriving with Mohammed, so I walked to class alone, and it just happened that I was the first to get there.

Mrs Bush's eyes lit up when I walked in. 'You're eager today, Cory James.'

I smirked as I sat in my usual seat, the same one I've sat in since year seven.

I pulled out my new pencil case and giant sketchpad as

Mrs Bush stood up from her desk to lock her classroom door.

I was slightly suspicious of why she'd locked us alone in her classroom, so I looked up at her as she walked over to me.

She whispered, 'I'm so glad you can finally wear makeup to school.' She shook her fist as if to say 'Victory!'

A light bulb went off inside my head.

Lizzie had wondered why Mrs Bush never said a word when Mr Harris was bullying me. It seemed as if she just stood there and let him speak down to me, but she had been collecting all the information this whole time.

'It was you who reported Mr Harris, wasn't it?' I whispered back.

She admitted it and carried on. 'I don't know if I can tell you this but I'm going to anyway.' Mrs Bush paused before explaining that Mr Harris had been let go. I felt awful, and she could tell I was starting to get upset. I told Mrs Bush that I had been wearing makeup even though I knew it was against the rules and that it was my fault he'd been sacked.

She shook her head in disbelief. 'You don't understand, Cory. How Mr Harris reacted to you was out of order; he was a bully.'

I repeated myself and said I should have never worn makeup if it was against the school's policy, and I didn't mean for anyone to get into trouble for doing their job. Mrs Bush leaned down to my level and placed her two hands on my shoulders. 'Listen to me. This is not your fault.' I just looked at the ground. I felt so responsible.

Then Mrs Bush added, 'Believe me, if you thought what Mr Harris said to your face was bad, you should have heard what he said when you weren't around. This is not your fault, only his.'

The classroom door handle rattled as it shook up and down. We both looked over, and Lizzie waved outside the door window. 'Um, I think the door is jammed?' Mrs Bush turned to me to quickly say, 'Don't mention this to anyone until it's made official.' I nodded. She walked over to the door and twisted the lock open. When Lizzie came in, she saw I looked uncomfortable, but she took it as if I was annoyed at her for taking so long. 'Jeeze, Cory, I couldn't help that I needed a wee. Stop being so clingy.' I apologised and agreed that I was being clingy.

The noise level soon rose as the classroom didn't take long to fill up.

Lizzie looked horrified. She held a can of Heinz tomato soup in her hand, whinging that the tin had been battered in her bag.

For Lizzie's GCSE composition, she chose to do her take on Andy Warhol's pop art, and she'd been sketching a can of soup. The sketch would be all out of proportion now that the tin was damaged.

I held out my hand. 'Let me see?' I turned the soup tin around to inspect it. 'Yeh, it is pretty damaged.' I chuckled.

Lizzie snatched it back from me. 'Don't laugh. What will I do now?'

'You could buy another one or choose something different?'

'Choose something different? I spent all last lesson outlining this.' She pointed at her half-sketched drawing.

While we were discussing soup-gate, in the background, disruptions were going on at the back of the class.

Mrs Bush marched past us to intervene. 'Boys! I'm going to have to split you up.' Mohammed was trying to paint Ben's face and made quite a mess over their desk.

'Ben, collect your belongings and sit next to Cory James.'

'Why, Mrs?' Ben asked, sounding slightly paranoid as to why she chose me of all people.

'It's been mentioned Cory has helped you with maths, so maybe Mr James can help you concentrate on art, too.'

'Really, Mrs?' Mohammed whinged as Ben rubbed the paint off his face using his sleeve.

And as instructed, Ben gathered his belongings and got up to sit next to me.

'Hello, you.' Ben spoke quietly, quickly glancing at me.

'Hey.' I looked forward, not making any eye contact.

Lizzie, on the other side of me, whispered, 'Cory, do you want me to switch seats with you? I'm brilliant at explaining how to draw.'

'Not a chance.' I grinned. Lizzie thought I secretly fancied Ben and didn't know we'd kissed.

I couldn't process that Mr Harris had been sacked. I didn't feel so guilty anymore now that Mrs Bush had reassured me, but the whole situation was playing on my mind.

Ben whispered, 'So what's up?' Could he sense that

something was wrong? I couldn't use the excuse that I was being clingy.

'Nothing.' I forced a smile, imagining that Ben might think I was nervous that he was next to me in class.

Ben's seat came increasingly closer during class, and then Ben's hand was on my leg. I felt cold as I shivered with nerves.

'I want to hold your hand,' Ben said quietly so no one else could hear.

I wanted to, so bad. I whispered back, 'What if we get caught?'

Ben said we wouldn't and then tapped my leg with his hand.

I slowly lowered my arm under the table and linked our palms. It felt like when he cuddled me while camping; I was excited but also nervous to be caught by anyone. I had also never held a boy's hand before. It felt good. My pulse was racing so much that I couldn't concentrate on my work. But no one had any idea. Everyone was too busy sketching or painting their object in front of them. Little did they know Ben Roberts and I were secretly holding hands under our table.

Ben mumbled, 'Better?' My heart was so whole that Ben wanted to hold my hand as he sensed I was upset about something.

'Sorry, I can't sketch,' I whispered to Ben as I switched hands with my pencil.

Ben whispered, 'We need to do that again soon.'

A smile spread across my face as I sketched.

After school, I was going around Ben's house for the first time, and his dad's car pulled up as he collected us from the school.

Trevor whizzed his big black range rover alongside the path, and his flashy car made everyone look over. 'Nice whip,' a student said.

When I climbed up inside the vehicle, it was like sitting inside a spaceship full of the latest car technology. I'm not usually a big fan of cars, but this was impressive. It even had heated seats and touch screens on the back of the passenger seats. His dad didn't acknowledge me though, and Ben had even introduced me as his friend who would help him pass GCSE Maths so he could go to the football academy, but he wasn't interested in me at all. I was slightly disappointed as I was meeting Ben's only parent; this was a big deal. I thought of how my mum was much warmer to Ben when she first met him. Why was Trevor being so icy?

Once we got inside Ben's house, there were pictures of his dad mainly playing football or holding trophies when he was a lot younger. There were hardly any pictures of Ben, which I thought was strange. Is Trevor a narcissist? I thought. Where are the images of his son?

Once we were upstairs, Ben beamed. 'I can't wait to show you my stuff.' Ben swung his bedroom door open, and I followed behind into his spacious room. It was the typical lad's bedroom with framed signed football T-shirts from footballers I had never heard of. But then, I only knew Cristiano Ronaldo and David Beckham. He gave me a full tour, including football medals and trophies, random photographs, and swimming certificates fixed on his wall with sticky tape.

Ben seemed so proud to show me around. 'What do you think?'

'Nice,' I replied. There was nothing inside this room that I could relate to, but strangely, I found it endearing as it was Ben's room.

'I want to show you something, but you're either going to think it's cute or super weird.'

'Okay?'

'Promise you won't think it's weird?'

We shook on it as I raised my pinky in the air.

'Promise.'

Ben pulled back his pillow, and a tiny picture of me was hiding underneath, cut out from our school year photo. It wasn't the best photo of me. I was not too fond of that picture as Mr Harris had made me wash off my makeup before the photoshoot.

'That's really cute.' I grabbed Ben's hands and leaned in to kiss.

'No, no, we can't do that here.' He pushed my chest back away from him.

'Sorry.'

Ben placed his pillow back over the photo.

'Trevor could walk in at any moment.'

'Won't your dad see that picture when changing the bedding?'

'I've done all my own washing since I was twelve.'

Ben walked to the room's other side and opened a mini fridge. 'Fancy a drink?'

I should have guessed he would have a mini fridge in his bedroom. Now I was impressed. I know it's my mum's payday when our kitchen fridge is full again, but here Ben was with his own bedroom fridge full of confectionary and soda cans. 'Here!' Ben chucked a

cold can of cola at me. I slowly opened it in case it

exploded all over his nice cream carpets.

'Ben!' Trevor shouted up the stairs.

'Coming, Dad. What does he want?' Ben placed his can

on his bedside table and explained he would return in a

second as he closed the door behind him. I had a peek

around Ben's room, looking at various things, then just

sat alone on his bed. I could hear his dad's loud voice

downstairs, so I slowly crept onto the landing so I could

listen much clearer. I could tell the conversation was

getting heated.

'Are you gay?'

'No, Dad.'

'Are you sure? Why are you bringing home a boy

wearing makeup?'

I could have kicked myself. I had forgotten to remove my makeup before leaving school and hadn't even realised. I didn't want to show Ben up in front of his dad. I looked across the hallway and saw a mirror hung up. I glanced at my sorry reflection looking back at me. For the first time in my life, I hated myself for wearing makeup, as I knew Ben would have cringed when he saw me on the way to meet his dad, but he was too nice to say anything. Then I heard something that didn't sound nice.

'Dad, he's just some freak from school.' My heart had officially been ripped out.

Ben continued, 'I'm just using him to help me get to the football academy, that's all.' I knew the whole thing had been too good to be true. Ben wasn't gay, he was pretending to be queer so I would continue to help him with his coursework.

Ever had a dream come true, and then in a moment, the whole thing is ripped away from you? Ben's words cut so sharply as the name 'freak' was a trigger for me. With this, I tiptoed down the stairs, my feet like jelly, but I managed to get down the stairs without falling or making noise and then slipped my school shoes back on.

They both said more things, but I couldn't bear to listen anymore, so I decided to make a run for it. I slowly pulled down the door handle without making a peep and opened the front door.

I couldn't help but think how Lizzie was right. Nothing good would come out of our unlikely friendship.

The front door slammed behind me, which Ben must have heard. I started running down his street with so many tears falling down my face that I couldn't see properly. He must have realised I had heard it all, but it was too late; I heard his voice shout my name as I turned a corner, and he must have come outside to find me long gone.

I didn't know the way off by heart, but I found my way as I saw familiar streets. It was pretty far away to run and walk, which made my school shoes rub my feet, but I didn't care; I wanted my feet to hurt more than my heart did.

Hearing Ben's poisonous words gave me a massive reality check. The first thing I did was block his number on my phone.

When I finally got home, everything since Ben called

me a freak was a blur. I couldn't even remember getting

home, and everything was a haze. I just ran to my room

and cried into the pillow on my bed. My mum followed

me into my room as she could hear me crying and

cuddled me as I sobbed. She didn't ask what was wrong,

but I think she knew deep down as I was supposed to be

at Ben's.

It was as if all the colour in my world was now grey, and

I just wanted the pain to stop hurting. If you looked at

me right then, you would have been able to see right

through to the other side as I had a hole in my chest

where my heart used to live.

It had been almost a week since I ran out of Ben's house, and I'd successfully been able to avoid him ever since. The truth was, I hadn't been able to talk to him as it still felt raw.

I got a text from Lizzie: Almost finished, ten minutes. She had a free lesson and was working on her soup masterpiece in Mrs Bush's class.

I sat on the usual bench as our break hour had just started, waiting for her to arrive.

Grabbing my attention, a magpie flew right in front of me and hopped around the grass. Great, I don't need any more sorrow, I thought.

'Shoo!' I got off the bench and chased the bird away. 'Shoo!' Then, I sat back on the bench once I was confident the bird had buggered off.

The plan was to go outside the school for lunch today and visit the local chippy. Lizzie's treat as she reckoned I needed cheering up after my fall out with Ben. She knew everything now, as I'd opened up about the whole Ben thing. I was pleasantly surprised when she didn't give a TED Talk about how she was right.

At the chippy, Lizzie will have her usual cheese, chips and gravy, which I find gross.

I mean, who mixes those three?

She forever calls me boring when I order my cone of chips – loaded with lots of salt and vinegar.

As I waited, I scrolled social media on my new phone. It wasn't as modern as my previous iPhone, but it'd do for now.

The worst thing about scrolling on social media was that I always saw happy gay couples; I wanted that. But

I was forever going to be single unless I ditched the makeup and changed who I was.

Not that I was ready for a relationship so soon after falling out with Ben. At the moment, I couldn't even listen to a love song or watch anything remotely to do with love or being in a relationship, as everything reminded me of Ben.

Engrossed in a video that had just gone viral, I felt someone sit close next to me.

'Hey, Liz–'

Turning to my side, I realised it was not Lizzie sitting next to me.

'I'll be quick. Just let me explain.' Ben's arms leaned on his legs, and he crouched forward while looking at me. His body and face were conflicted, like my heart and head. His stature exuded confidence, but I could tell he was a rabbit in headlights by his facial mannerisms.

I unzipped my bag's side pocket and stored my phone safely inside. As I stood up from Ben, he pursued to carry on. 'I'm sorry for whatever you overheard, Cory.'

I turned my back and walked away from the only guy I'd ever been infatuated with.

'You don't know what it's like being me.'

I shook my head with disbelief. 'No, Ben, don't go there.' I made a U-turn and walked back over to him, my face on fire with rage.

Ben tried to apologise. 'I needed to throw my dad off. I never meant any of it.'

'This needs to stop. We need to stop, Ben.'

'Why?'

'Because I'm going to get hurt.'

Ben stood up and walked over to me. He gripped my expressive arms to calm me down. I pulled away and carried on: 'You're not even out. You're one of the football boys, and then there's me. Boys like me don't–' We were interrupted.

A group of year seven girls walked past us and giggled out loud annoyingly. They weren't laughing at us, but laughter contrasted our private moment. We waited until they finally passed us so we could continue our conversation, which was becoming heated.

Ben huffed, 'You don't know–'

'Don't you dare say "I don't know what it's like being you." You will never know what it's like to be a boy in makeup. You get to hide, and I don't, Ben.'

Ben's voice raised. 'So you're pressuring me to come out?'

My voice shook as I calmly explained, 'No, I'm saying...

I don't want to be your secret anymore.'

Ben leaned back on the bench, but his body language

wasn't confident this time.

I hadn't been to the chippy with Lizzie in those ten

minutes, but I still walked away with a chip on my

shoulder.

Ben

The following Friday, I gathered a handful of my

football mates, including my best friend, Mohammed,

into the school library. It was the day before our most

important match yet, the one that was going to be

broadcast live on channel S4C. The lads turned up, and

they didn't look too pleased, as I could sense they were nervous about my announcement.

Mo looked up before he started. 'You better not be quitting the team, Roberts.' I was acting jittery and asked the boys to sit on the chairs in front of me.

'Umm, there's something I've got to announce, boys,' I stuttered. I swallowed to carry on, but my mouth was parched. This sort of thing always happened if I had to speak in front of a class. For some reason, my nerves drained me and my ability to speak.

'Don't think about it,' Mo said on the topic of quitting.

'No, no, it's not that.' I glanced at a few of the boys, who looked at each other, seemingly relieved. I felt their victory would be short-lived when I explained the real reason.

I paced around in a circle and tried to get my words out, but it felt like having to jump off the side of a building blindfolded.

Was it a big jump?

Would I be hurt?

Was I about to die?

I could hear my heart racing so loudly that it was beating in my ears.

I tiptoed towards the edge of the building, not knowing what was going to be at the other end. I have to jump, I thought. I have to leap forward.

I took a deep breath, and then I jumped.

'I'm gay.'

Complete silence.

'Right, and?' one of them said.

The reaction made the jump feel like more of a small step forward.

'No, I'm being serious. I really do like boys.'

'Fine. And what did you call us all here to tell us?' Mo added, raising one eyebrow.

I felt like no one was listening. I found myself questioning; why weren't they beating me up or calling me names?

I stood on a chair and shouted across the library, 'I. LOVE. MEN!'

'Get down and be quiet. This is a library, Ben,' the school librarian whispered angrily, pointing at me like I was a naughty five-year-old.

'If you've called us to tell us that you like boys, we don't care. It has nothing to do with football.'

'Wait, you can still play football if you're gay, right?' Mo asked innocently.

I wasn't being cocky, but I knew I was one of their valuable players. I was elated with their reactions, and if I'd only known it was this easy, I would have done it a lot sooner, and then maybe I wouldn't have lost Cory. I'd never suffered from anything like depression before, but that's how I felt now that Cory wouldn't forgive me. I cried all the time and only wanted to go to my bed. Cory was lucky he could talk to his mum or his friend Lizzie, but I was suffering alone.

This made me decide to come out, as I didn't want to pretend I was someone else anymore. I wanted my friends to know the real Ben.

I nodded to Mo's question. 'Of course I can still play football. I just wanted to be honest with you boys.'

Mo got up and gave me a massive bro hug. He could tell I was exhausted from working myself up. He said what I had done took real guts, and the other boys agreed and commended me for it.

'You're safe here, bro,' Mo added. We had been best friends since we were little, and Mo said he could never disown his friend for something so trivial as being gay. Mo thought it would be like not being friends with someone just because they didn't like the same colour or food as you, which would be ridiculous.

And then the other boys joined in, and they all group-hugged me. Boys being boys, some scratched my flustered head and play-fought, jabbing me in my side. After falling out with Cory, I didn't think my smile would ever return.

But today, I smiled, I felt safe, and for the first time in fifteen years, I finally felt free.

Cory

While Ben took a small step forward and a giant step for gay men in sports, I turned around a hallway corner when a year-nine girl approached me. The girl was taller than me, a pretty brunette with big brown eyes.

'Are you the LGBTQ+ school ambassador?' she said confidently.

'That's me.'

'I'm Jenny. Do you mind if we go somewhere private for a chat?' I had never had another student approach me regarding LGBTQ+ issues before, so I was excited to help. The canteen was quiet during this time of day, so we headed there and sat at a table that wasn't near

anyone else. Jenny sat next to me.

'So how can I help?' I asked.

'Well, I'm trans and great at netball.'

'Okay?'

'Well, I'm worried about applying for the school's team

as I don't want any backlash for being trans. I'm going

through a lot at the moment so I could do without any

added negativity.'

I tried to reassure Jenny that people are much more

open-minded these days and that it should be fine to try

out for the netball team.

'For gay boys maybe, but trans people are always under

fire, especially participating in sports.' Jenny educated

me on how some people think it's unfair for trans girls

to play on a female team as they believe people assigned

male at birth are genetically stronger than those assigned female.

I wasn't aware of this issue. I knew Cartridge was becoming more accepting of diversity, though, so I was confident it would be okay, and I would try to support her if there were any challenges.

'I just want to play netball, like any other girl on the team,' Jenny stressed.

'You will.'

'So you don't think being trans will go against me applying?'

'It's no one's business if you want to play sports, only yours.'

"I always try to be twice as good as anyone else as I've never been taken seriously, but when I beat the other girls, they blame it on the gender I was assigned.'

'Out of interest, how has your experience been at this school as a trans girl?'

'The school has been okay. Year seven and eight were tough as some stupid girls wouldn't let me use the women's toilets. I would have to wait until I got home, which was painful.'

'That's awful. How did you get them to let you?'

'I didn't. Mrs Powell did.'

'She did?' I smiled.

'Yes, she's been brilliant recently. I was actually looking at moving school until she intervened with the bullying.'

I felt awful about Jenny's earlier experience but also warm, as it was typical of Mrs Honey to make a difference.

She added, 'School is not too bad now, though. But I'm also fostered, so I have to get permission from social services for any medication, which can be a bit of a headache.' Jenny explained that her foster carer has been like a mother to her and championed social services to get Jenny on hormone blockers. I felt like I had known Jenny for longer than the ten minutes we had spoken, maybe because she was so open about her experience. I left the conversation thinking of what an inspiration she was; she probably had been bullied her whole life for being trans and had to fight to be who she was. Plus, it mustn't be easy being in the care system, either.

'Go and apply for the netball team, Jen. You've come too far in your life to let other people's opinions affect what you love doing.'

'You give good advice, and I guess I feel more sensitive

than usual after finding out today that my favourite author, I.B. Trolling, might be a TERF.'

'I.B. Trolling, doesn't she go under a man's pen name now? I guess it's okay to pose as a man if it's to sell books,' I said sarcastically.

'Yes!' Jenny agreed. 'You've been great, Cory.' And we hugged.

'Good luck!'

And that's when Jenny made her way to the sports board to put her name forward for the upcoming netball trials. I was starting to enjoy the ambassador role. It made me begin to enjoy school more, too, as it gave me a purpose. The news about Mr Harris was also official; I was glad when it was explained why he'd been removed as I wouldn't want the likes of Lewis Jackson to push any narrative that it was my fault.

Now that I understood that Mr Harris was targeting me, I was relieved he had been dismissed, and I allowed myself not to feel guilty about it anymore.

Despite finally enjoying school, I thought about Ben all day, every day.

At my house the next day, approximately three minutes before Ben's big game started, Lizzie and I were snuggled under a throw, spread out on the living room sofa and munching on popcorn, anticipating the start of the big game.

My mum rummaged in her purse to find a one-pound coin to slot into the back of the TV but thought she might have used it this morning when Ryan was watching CBeebies.

'It's here, somewhere!' she said as she picked out some change to get a better view. 'Got it!' She walked over to the TV, almost falling over one of Ryan's toy cars. 'I told you to put this away!' Michelle snapped, looking over to Ryan, who was in his own world and, annoyingly, making a lot of racket as he crashed with his noisy train set.

'Choo-choo! Crash!'

The number of hours left on the TV changed from 00:23 to 04:23 as Michelle dropped the coin into the pay-as-you-view metre.

'Cheers, Mum.'

'Can't have the TV run out. Imagine that as Ben scores a goal.'

I was annoyed my mum thought I was only watching for Ben.

Was I only watching to see Ben?

I told myself I didn't want to be the only person from school not watching the match today. The school was buzzing for Ben and Mo's big game today; they even posted about it on our school's social media accounts, which they didn't typically do for outside school events.

They had yet to post about the upcoming pride event even though we're taking part as a school.

'Do you guys want anything to drink?' Michelle asked, but we politely declined, and she picked up Ryan from the floor and encouraged him to come and play in his room.

'Shall we give Cory and Lizzie some quiet for the game?' she said as they left the living room. I was thankful, as I knew the noise would have distracted us, or Ryan would be asking me to help him play halfway through.

The commercial break finished, and the program started. I've never been one to watch football, so I felt more masculine as the theme tune began to play in the introduction. I dug my hands into the popcorn dish, grabbing the world's record for most popcorn in one's hand ever.

'Dun-dun, da dun-dun.' Lizzie began to hum.

I looked at Lizzie, absolutely stunned. 'Didn't realise you watched footie.'

'I love it.'

What a revelation, I thought as I filled my mouth with popcorn.

Two commentators, Nigel and Dave, greeted viewers and introduced themselves as the program started. I think they were both from Oldport, but their accents sounded much thicker on TV. Like Ant and Dec, I wouldn't be able to point out which one was which if anyone were to ask.

The two men bounced off each other as they presented the game.

'This should be an excellent game with Oldport against Swansea.'

'A really tough encounter for Oldport, but a clean sheet could be massive.'

'Last August, wasn't it? The last clean sheet.'

'Yeh.'

Other than the commentators, you could also hear a roaring noise from the stadium as there weren't many empty seats as so many people came to watch the teams play. It gave me a sense of FOMO because I bet the atmosphere would have been electric in real life.

Then the stadium erupted with cheers, and we watched as the Swansea boys walked out onto the pitch first.

Lizzie was drooling as they were much beefier than the Oldport guys.

'They're going to get smashed by those other players. Look at the size of them,' Lizzie added, grabbing the popcorn from me before I devoured it all.

The commentators continued.

'Here come the Oldport boys.'

'Lots of fans cheering Oldport County until I die.'

'Yes, and bizarrely, there's a roar of laughter from the crowds.'

'Is it a streaker again?'

'Not sure just yet.'

'A small man is now running across the pitch.'

'Let's hope it's not a streaker.' Both commentators laughed.

'It's football coach Trevor Roberts. He appears angry.'

Lizzie and I perched up on the sofa as if it would help us see better. It's not that I wanted to see Ben's dad streaking, but I didn't want Ben to be embarrassed by his dad.

'This is a circus. Trevor Roberts is running after a player; neither are naked, may I add.'

'Phew,' said Nigel, wiping his forehead.

'What is going on?' Lizzie stood up and yelled at the TV.

'This is the beauty of live TV, folks,' Nigel said.

'The ref is now whistling, asking Trevor to leave the pitch. Crowds are booing Trevor Roberts. It's all very savage here.'

They both laughed. 'Talking of savage, Dave. Lily Savage is on the pitch!'

We gasped as we realised what was going on in the stadium.

Lipstick, blusher, false lashes and everything in

between.

Ben was the boy in makeup.

The boys looked pleased with their medals. The

commentator, Nigel, asked a few questions, and the

boys responded confidently.

'You're playing against Cheltenham next week. Could

this be a winning streak after today's performance?' The

microphone was placed in front of Ben.

'Absolutely.' Ben smiled.

'And why the makeup, Ben?'

Mohammed interrupted and grabbed the mic. 'Well,

Nigel, Ben came out to us as gay. We want to tell our

supporters that if they attack him because of it, they're

attacking us as a team.'

'Yeah!' The team cheered.

Lizzie turned up the volume on the TV remote and shouted, 'Ben came out!'

My mum came down the stairs with Ryan. 'What was that?' But I was too engrossed in the television to respond.

The reporter smiled. 'But Ben, why the need for makeup to tell everyone that you're gay?'

The camera focused on Ben, and we all glared at the tv. He had removed the false eyelashes and looked even more handsome on TV.

'Because someone I hurt doesn't think I understand what it's like being a guy who wears makeup.'

Mo grabbed the mic. 'Cory lad, forgive him, for god's sake.'

'Cory, forgive the lad,' Nigel said, looking into the camera as he ended his segment.

We all screamed at the TV, jumping up and down with little Ryan looking at us confused.

When I heard Ben mention me on TV, I had mixed emotions. I felt so happy as I couldn't believe Ben did that for me, and it could risk his career and reputation if this didn't go down well. And what would his dad say?

My mum announced, 'Right. We're going down to the stadium.'

'We are?' I asked. I started playing with my hair, brushing it to one side as if it would make it look any better.

'Yes,' she shouted as she ran upstairs to get changed.

'Really?' I shouted back, fidgeting with my fingers.

'Yes, Cory, you have to go,' said Lizzie.

I smirked as I watched Ben's face on TV. I was also grateful for Lizzie as I was ditching our day at mine to catch Ben, but, being my good friend, she wanted me to go.

'Lizzie, are you sure it's fine?' I said, heading out to the hallway to slide my shoes on.

'You go. I'll mind Ryan for your mum.' Mum seemed in a hurry to leave the house, and getting Ryan out of his pyjamas and hurdling through crowds probably wouldn't be a great idea.

I laced my shoes up and gave my best friend a massive hug.

'You're my best friend, Lizzie.'

'I know.' Lizzie smiled warmly.

My mum climbed the stairs and flung the keys off the wall as I threw my coat on.

Lizzie smiled and waved me off as we ran to the car.

'Get your boy!'

The small blue Nissan rattled on the gravel as my mum pulled off.

Once we left Oldport, the traffic was typical for a game day but even worse because road works were going on. I was never going to catch Ben at this rate. I pulled my phone out to unblock Ben's number, and it was the first time I had rang his number since our falling out.

'This is Ben. Please leave a message after the beep'.

BEEP!

My mum listened in to see if Ben would answer.

'Any luck, love?'

'Not yet, Mum.'

I tried again, but still no answer.

During our car journey, my mum admitted that she always knew something was happening between us since the day she met Ben.

She also gave a side-eye to the time she had to collect us from the campsite and found me alone with Ben sharing a sleeping bag.

'I can see why you'd think that, but nothing was happening during that time.'

'Sure it wasn't.' Michelle exhaled.

'Honest.'

'And when you were hysterical about breaking your phone?'

'Okay, you've got me there.' I started to laugh. I didn't think my mum knew what was going on, but it seems what they say about mums is true – they know everything.

'I've always liked Ben, and that's why I never had a problem with him coming around, as he's a good lad. Very charming and respectful.'

It made me beam with pride to get my mum's approval of Ben. She hadn't had a chance to tell me what she really thought of him, as when we fell out, I didn't want to talk about him anymore.

The car moved down the road sluggishly as the traffic didn't seem to be progressing very fast.

Once we got closer, I instructed my mum to pull over the car, knowing I could run faster than we were moving.

'You sure?' Michelle asked. She knew it was a good fifteen-minute walk from the stadium. And as always, it was also pouring rain. Typical bloody British weather. 'See you later. Love you.' I slammed the passenger door shut.

I put my hood up and ran towards the crowds of people coming in my direction. Getting anywhere fast was difficult as so many fans were coming out. I was flustered, and the rain was getting heavier. I ducked between shop doorways where there was shelter, but I had to be quick; time was against me. As I ran, I was mindful of how slippery the ground had become. It would be just my luck to have a broken arm just for running in the rain.

As I got closer, I saw the gigantic football stadium in front of me, which strangely looked like a big tent with yellow horns. I still needed to determine where the boys

would be coming out from; the oddly shaped building

was massive, but I presumed they'd be exiting from the

backdoors... Wherever that was.

I saw someone who looked like they might work at the

stadium.

'Excuse me, where is the exit the footballers will be

coming out from?' I asked. They turned to me with

their HiVis jacket on and hood up.

'Nice try. But we don't give that information to fans.'

Uh, fans? I'm not a fan, I thought. But they wouldn't

believe me.

I huffed as I walked farther down the road. The boys

had to be coming out from somewhere, and I hoped I

was early and hadn't missed them, as I wouldn't know if

they'd already come out.

I saw a coach parked up much farther down, and as I got closer, I could see Mohammed and a few of the boys running into their coach, and then I saw Ben. I had caught them!

'Ben! Ben!' I shouted. I tried to run faster, but I got a stitch, so I had to stop for a moment. Then the bus pulled off, and I hurled over, clenching my stomach. I was approximately three minutes too late.

One of the boys at the back of the bus must have noticed me hurdled over as the coach drove past. The coach driver had no option but to pull over even though it was now on double yellow lines. The coach hissed as it came to a stop. Ben waited for the doors to open before running towards the crowds, and the coach drove away.

Ben ran towards me in the pouring rain, calling my name. I ignored the stomach cramp and attempted to run towards him. We got closer, and both smiled as Ben opened his arms to hold me.

The crowds walking past moved out of the way as we got close to each other. And when our lips touched, it felt like we levitated over the masses into the sky. Untouchable, safe and like nothing else in the world mattered.

It was cinematic and dramatic, exactly like a Hollywood movie, except in this blockbuster, we weren't a straight couple.

The pouring rain thoroughly showered us. Tiny river flows of glitter and rainbow colours dripped down our faces. We were no longer the boys in makeup; nature exposed our true natural beauty as our lips locked.

We weren't aware of the football fans walking by as no one else at this moment mattered, just us. Our eyes focused only on each other.

Both of my hands held Ben's as we passionately kissed; like always, his hands were warmer than mine.

A football hooligan shouted "Faggots!" while passing us. They said it again and this time threw a can of beer at us, but it missed.

We didn't even flinch, Ben's hands gripping mine tighter as we heard the remarks. The can of beer just rolled on the ground beside us.

Clenching his hands tighter into mine, I whispered into Ben's ear, 'I know you don't like being saved, but I've got you.'

'And you've got me, too.'

Then, I wrapped my arms around Ben and held him close for a few seconds. Oh, how I've missed him, I thought. I also missed his scent; as always, he smelt so masculine.

When Ben pulled away, he wiped the rain from my face.

'I never meant to upset you.'

'Me neither.'

'I never used you for maths. I told my dad that as he was suspicious,' Ben explained.

'I know.'

Rain trickled down Ben's face. 'No, you don't. You see, I pretended to be bad at maths so I'd have an excuse to be near you.'

My eyes started to fill up.

'I don't know if you're crying or if it's the rain.' He wiped my eyes with his hoodie sleeve.

'I thought you did it to get into the football academy?'

'It wasn't that. I just needed to be near you. I'll do anything to be around you, Cory. I would choose you over football any day.'

I felt like he had chosen me over football today, as Ben would know that his reputation would be compromised by pulling a stunt on the pitch that involved his personal life. We still didn't know how people would react, the fans and football scouts and what opportunities might not happen due to today's stunt. But Ben didn't care; he said he felt like he had scored because we were together again.

We were making out again when a familiar voice interrupted us.

'Put him down, Ben. You don't know where he's been!'

Michelle stood with a large umbrella. We both smiled at

my mum as she came to shelter us from the bad

weather.

'Let's get you home, boys.'

I tapped Go LIVE.

I was back with my usual 'get ready with me' LIVE stream, and so was the gremlin in my stomach. It didn't matter how often I did these things; I never got more confident or less anxious.

'Hey, everyone,' I began. 'It's been a minute, so if you want to ask me any questions, just fire away.'

Like always, I paused to wait for more people to join before I answered questions. I glanced over my shoulder, and Ben was lying on my bed. One hand was placed under his head, and the other was gripping his phone.

Even though Ben's football team and most people from school had been so positive about him coming out, his dad was still coming to terms with his son being gay.

Ben apologised to his dad on the night of the big

football match and came out properly, but apparently,

Trevor didn't take it too well.

Ben explained Trevor was a lot quieter around him

these days, and sometimes I caught Ben checking his

phone to see if his dad had rung or messaged, but

there's always nothing.

Ben noticed I was looking at him. 'Just pretend I'm not

here, babe.'

I loved it when he called me babe, and I much preferred

it to my other nickname that he was trying to make

happen: Hunky-Cory. I mean, I was anything but

hunky. He did it all the more now he knew it made my

toes curl.

'You're not putting me off, don't worry,' I said as I

turned to face my mobile screen. In front of me, there

was a row of makeup lined up on my desk, from moisturiser to mascara. Of course, it wasn't me that was this tidy; Ben organised it as he said it would help me as I do my live feed. He's good like that, always making things more shiny and perfect.

Cory, I love your makeup looks! one follower called BillieEilishFan12 wrote.

'BillieEilishFan12, thanks.' I smiled.

Are you staying on at Cartridge High? asked a pupil from school.

'I am, actually.' I paused for a brief second. 'I love that school!' And I did. I was so proud to be from Cartridge; sure, it wasn't the most attractive school, but it had heart.

I quickly applied my Ordinary moisturiser as I also needed to get Ben ready after I finished; there was a big event today – Pride.

Another viewer asked, Hey, Cory, do you have a boyfriend?

It was the most common question I was always asked during these Q&As.

'No, I don't have a boyfriend, but I am seeing someone.'

I was still waiting for Ben to make it official. I figured it was best to wait for Ben to ask me, as he'd only just come out, so I didn't want to rush him. And my insecure side questioned if he actually wanted to be my boyfriend.

Ben paused playing a football game on his phone and came up from behind me.

'This is Ben.' I smiled as he kissed me on my cheek. I was surprised he came on camera and gave PDA, as he'd never done it before, but he'd been much more confident since coming out. The live feed was overwhelmed with lovely comments, and some asked if Ben had a TikTok page. He didn't, as Ben hated social media, especially since he read negative tweets written about him wearing makeup at the big game. Some Oldport football supporters believed Ben was unprofessional in bringing his love life into the sport, and quite a few homophobic jokes were posted, too. Ben considered being active on specific platforms harmful to mental health, but on the live feed, he politely apologised as he didn't have TikTok.

'Ben has been accepted with Cartridge High's football academy in the sixth form,' I announced.

The feed was so busy that my outdated iPhone made the stream lag and break up all the time.

It was frustrating as I needed to stream as quickly as possible, and the lag caused me to repeat myself multiple times. Eventually, I said goodbye and apologised for ending it so soon.

I tapped End Feed and unclipped my phone from the tripod.

Once I finished my makeup, Ben asked me to apply rainbow hearts on his cheeks using different coloured glitter eyeliners. I didn't mind as it wasn't too intricate to do, and I could finish it quickly.

I gripped Ben's head with one hand. 'Stop moving, Ben.' I was trying my best to concentrate and do a good job.

Ben giggled like a little boy. 'It's tickling my cheek.'

Using glitter eyeliner was perfect because it meant there would be no fall out from the glitter, and it had a built-in glue to secure it to his skin. 'There you go,' I said, handing Ben a handheld mirror.

'Tidy!'

'But you didn't even look properly.'

Ben picked up the mirror again. 'Yeh, it's perfect.' He grinned.

Ben wasn't bothered about having makeup on, so I could have scribbled anything on his face, and he'd be his laid-back self and say, 'Tidy'.

Ben may have been chirpy, but I wasn't feeling like myself.

I didn't need a mood ring, I had a face. And this was how Ben could read that something was bothering me today.

'Right, are you going to tell me what's up?' Ben's still sat down, and he pulled me between his legs.

I exhaled and told Ben everything was fine, but I knew I didn't sound convincing. Ben said my face looked like I was overthinking something.

Ben opened his arms. 'Come here.' He wrapped himself around me and then held me tightly. He whispered in my ear, 'What's up, babe?'

While he was cwtching me without eye contact, I explained that I felt like I forced Ben to come out. When argued by the school bench, I said he didn't know what it was like being a boy in makeup and that one of the reasons we couldn't work was because I didn't want to be his secret. Since he came out, I'd felt I pushed him to do it, and he wouldn't have done it if I hadn't forced him to. I wished he had done it on his own accord, in his own time.

Ben pulled away, and his eyes widened. 'You forced me? I was worried I had put you in a position where you were pressured to forgive me.'

I shook my head. 'No way, I I–'

I paused before I accidentally said the word 'love', but I carried on: 'I like you a lot.'

'I like you a lot, too,' Ben said, lighting up the room with his pearly whites.

I let the idea sink in that we both had been worrying about the other person when we didn't have to.

'Why do we act this way?' I smiled at Ben.

'Because we both care.' He kissed my forehead. 'So do me a favour, stop worrying, yeh?'

Ben pulled his phone out of his pocket to check the
time, and his phone lock screen was a picture of us, a
selfie with Ben kissing my check while I laughed. A bit
like how we were on the LIVE feed.

'Shit, is that the time? Pride is in an hour! We better get
a move on, Cory,'

Notifications from his dad? Still zero.

At the pride event, we met up with Lizzie, Mohammed
and some of the students from school. I was glad Lizzie
dragged herself out to take part. I knew she hated the
build-up of public events, which seemed to trigger her
social anxiety, but she always ended up enjoying it when
she was there.

'Wow, these look great,' I said as I pulled a T-shirt out
of a bag. Lizzie had used her mum's Cricut machine to

make Cartridge High Pride T-shirts with today's date, August 8th 2023, and they were black with glitter rainbow text. The sun was already starting to heat the back of my neck. Luckily, we chose to wear T-shirts today as we would have definitely roasted in jumpers or hoodies.

Loaded with fancy cold Frappuccinos, we changed into our T-shirts before we located one of the event coordinators on Oldport's high street.

Our march would be in front of the Barclays float and behind an ocean-themed float with gorgeous women dressed as rainbow-coloured mermaids. 'I'm not standing in front of these gorgeous women,' Lizzie whinged as she crossed her arms.

Mo was standing next to Ben and said, 'Hey Lizzie, I would rather see you up there shaking your thing.' He winked. It didn't come off as a joke but as if

Mohammed with flirting with Lizzie.

Lizzie would have normally berated Mo for saying

something that objectifies women, but her face lit up

like she enjoyed the compliment.

Once we lined up in our positions, Lizzie and I were at

the front, and Ben was with his team far behind.

'Just to brief you guys, there might be people shouting

phobic abuse, just ignore it and carry on if so,' the

organiser notified us.

Lizzie looked at me. 'Uh, what does that mean, Cory?'

She was the most nervous person the organiser could

have said it in front of.

I grabbed Lizzie's hand. 'You'll be fine.' I smiled

reassuringly.

'Will it be like the march in Hairspray? We're going to get locked up?' Lizzie's eyes looked petrified.

I reassured Lizzie that it was no longer the sixties, and she was no Tracy Turnblad.

An organiser with a walkie-talkie got a message saying the parade was about to start and gave us the green light to start moving. 'YMCA' by the Village People started playing loudly, and we could hear the crowds cheering as the first float moved in front. The parade was so colourful, and bright confetti burst across the street. Rainbow-coloured buntings draped between the high street shops. And we started to walk forward.

'This is it, guys,' Lizzie shouted. Lizzie and I lifted a banner with Cartridge High love all written on it, which was already a bad idea as I was dying to do the actions of the YMCA as everyone else joined in.

Lizzie and I made up for the lack of hand movement as we sang at the top of our lungs, 'It's fun to stay at the...' Behind us were our teachers waving mini Pride flags. It was strange to see them wearing regular clothes like the T-shirts made by Lizzie, regular jeans and trainers. Teachers were actually ordinary people outside of school – who would have thought?

Then, behind the teachers, came other year eleven pupils, including Lewis, who had a face like thunder. He'd been made to participate by Mr Waters after Lewis had been caught smoking on school grounds. Lewis only agreed so he wouldn't have suspension if he took part today. Poor Lewis, he looked like this was absolute torture for him. The other pupils clapped along to the music and smiled at the crowds. Behind year eleven was Ben's football team. You could hear them before seeing them as they made lots of noise with their rainbow-coloured whistles. When the crowds saw the football boys, they cheered even louder as many recognised them.

So many people came out to support and watch, and after all those years of worrying about being myself, I felt so loved and accepted at that moment. My eyes started to fill, and my cheeks ached from smiling too much. There's something quite special about being in the same place as many other people who have faced similar issues as you; we were all different, but we were all united.

Talking of uniting, one of the footballers nudged Ben's arm as he spotted Trevor standing in the crowd. Ben was shocked to see Trevor was there to support him, as he had been so cold since he came out and hadn't mentioned coming along to today's Pride. Trevor looked slightly awkward to be there, and it was out of character for him to attend, but he smiled softly and slowly waved a Pride flag in the air.

Ben left the march and went straight over to his dad. As he got closer, his dad could see his eyes filling up. Ben had never seen an emotional Trevor before.

As Ben got near his dad, Trevor held out his arms and wrapped his hand over the back of Ben's head as his once-little boy sobbed into his shoulder.

People next to the pair didn't watch on as it was obviously a private moment between father and son. The music was so loud, not that they needed to say anything, as Trevor showing love and acceptance was all that Ben needed.

Trevor kissed Ben's forehead and then pulled Ben away from him.

That was Ben's cue to join back in the parade; Trevor moved his head sideways, miming the words 'Go on'.

Ben's eyes were heavy, but he smiled before he made his way to catch up with the football boys.

I was pleased for Ben as I knew it would have meant a lot to see his dad cheering him on at Pride.

My family was also in the crowds. My mum had brought Trudy, who, typically, wore a T-shirt that read: I loves the gays.

Ryan had the cutest top that read: My brother is gay. Get over it.

And then I saw another familiar face: Jenny from year nine, and she joined us in the parade walk as YMCA was coming to an end.

She came alongside me. 'Cory,' she shouted, 'I did it! I got on the netball team.'

'Yass, girl, I knew you would,' I shouted back. I would have given her a supportive hug if I weren't holding up this bloody banner, but my legs were jumping with joy. I could feel the high spirits and positivity exuding from the crowds as we walked past; we saw many scantily clad people, dogs with pride tees and adorable children with same-sex parents.

As we got to the finish line, I was still holding the banner with Lizzie, and it was like we were winners of a TV talent show as chunky rainbow glitter dropped from the sky and 'Come So Far (Got So Far To Go)' from the musical Hairspray started playing.

'What a coincidence, it's Hairspray!' Lizzie shouted.

'I love this one!' I responded.

The whole parade sang along, and the atmosphere was incredible.

After the parade finished, we all took pictures for memories and our school's social media.

Most people left quite soon after the parade finished; Lizzie had got a lift with my family but Trudy, Ben and I planned on staying longer to check out some of the stalls.

After Ben finished saying goodbye to his team, he headed over to me. I was standing on my own, engrossed in my phone, swiping across and looking at the pictures from today's event.

Ben jabbed me in my side. 'Hey, Hunky-Cory.' And usually, I'd roll my eyes at the nickname, but my eyes were focused only on Ben.

'Hey.' I smirked as I slid my phone into my pocket. I then put my hand around his waist; his football T-shirt felt so silky, and Ben smelt so good, too. Like a mixture of masculinity and fresh fabric softener.

Ben rubbed his thumb over my nose softly. It was as if he was removing the cream from my Frappuccino.

'What is it?' I asked.

'I think it's burnt from the sun.'

I didn't think I needed extra sun protection today as my foundation had SPF. Ben suggested we should find a pharmacy to get some sun factor or aftersun cream. I thought it was cute that he was trying to care for me, but I said it would be fine.

Ben raised his eyebrows and looked dead serious. 'It's not fine. We're finding a Boots.' I mimicked what he had just said and told him how much I loved it when he looked so serious.

But he didn't respond, and we were just smirking at each other.

'Today has made me realise that I'm so lucky you came into my life,' Ben said, slowly moving his index finger up and down my arm. 'You know, I've never been as happy until I started being around you.'

'You've completely changed my world too,' I said, looking up at Ben.

Rainbow confetti continued sporadically sprinkling from the sky as Ben said, 'You do realise I would have never worn makeup for anyone else.'

'And I wouldn't have taken my makeup off for anyone else.' I smirked.

And then our lips touched as if we were the only ones

standing on the high street. People surrounding us

paused and started nudging and pointing as we

passionately made out in the closed road. When we

finally stopped, they all clapped and wolf-whistled.

Confetti was still trickling down from above us.

Ben smiled at me. He looked the happiest I'd ever seen.

His head dipped as he whispered into my ear.

'Cory James, will you be my boyfriend?'

Follow the Author to be notified when the next book is released!

ANTHONY CONNORS ROBERTS

@anthonyconnorsroberts

@anthonyconnorsroberts

Facebook.com/
AnthonyConnorsRoberts

www.anthonyconnorsroberts.com

If you enjoyed Cory and Ben's story, please leave a quick review on Amazon/Goodreads, as it will really help Anthony reach more readers like yourself.

SUPER-READABLE

This book uses the British Dyslexia Association guidelines to facilitate ease of reading. Adopting these principles for those with dyslexia has the advantage of making this story more accessible.

The text is printed in a larger-than-typical font, with wider character spacing and written in simple clear language, using everyday words.
It's purposely printed on cream paper, as some readers with vision deficiencies might find white too dazzling.

Also, as advised by BDA, the front cover is printed in matt, not gloss and uses a single-coloured background.

Happy reading!

Printed in Great Britain
by Amazon